not so merry memories

USA TODAY BESTSELLING AUTHOR
MEAGAN BRANDY

Edited by: Rebecca @ Fairest Reviews Editing Services
Edited by: Ellie McLove @ My Brother's Editor
Cover Design By: Jay Aheer @ Simply Defined Art

Want to be notified about future books releases of mine?
Sign up for my Newsletter today: Meagan Brandy's
Newsletter Sign Up

DEDICATION

*To the one who refuses to wait
for their happily ever after, but instead
takes it by the belt.*

And then ties them up with it...

SYNOPSIS

I've tried to forget him.
He refuses to allow it.

Now, here we are, forced to spend the holidays
together, pretending everything is as merry as
ever.

It isn't.
I know this.
He knows this.

Everyone else? Not so much thanks to the man
determined to be mine.
Despite all that's happened between us, he swears
not everything has changed.

He might be right…

CHAPTER 1

❄

N oel

Have you ever sat back and wondered what life would be like if you made one decision differently? Ever wished a memory away or prayed for a redo?

If you have... I can say with utmost certainty that you, you wishful thinker, are most definitely the asshole who made the mistake, and the time you would like to teleport back to is the moment you slid your average-size eggplant inside your girlfriend's roommate!

"Someone has a lot on her mind."

Never in my life have I slapped my laptop shut

so fast, my glare slicing over my shoulder and slamming into the eyes of the man who makes me wish I had ice cream for breakfast... so I could puke it up all over his impeccably polished shoes.

"And someone else is, yet again, speaking on things that do not concern them." Hooking my heel around the back leg of my chair, I spin until I'm facing him. Legs crossed, I drum my fingertips along the thick leather beneath my palm. "Why are you here?"

Arms folded over his stupidly broad chest, he cocks his head like the condescending asshole he is. "What were you writing?"

"My speech for the opening."

"That'll go over well with potential buyers." He doesn't miss a beat, this one, eyes always sharp and assessing.

"I'm sure their wives will relate beautifully." My smile is a sugary sham as I push to stand, blindly grabbing my laptop and sliding it into my bag. I wipe the fake away. "I know the whole 'couple thing' is a foreign concept to you, but why do you think I suggested a couples conference?" I lift a brow, taking two steps forward and answering before he has a chance. "When a husband assumes his wife is uncomfortable or appears a little less naïve than he assumed her to be, said husband will open his wallet."

"My wallet is plenty big enough now."

"And apparently, so is your ego."

I shoulder past the man, but I'm caught by an arm, halting me at his side.

My gaze darts to his.

"So sassy these days," he accuses.

"Gee." I tip my head. "I wonder why that is."

"The man with the average-size eggplant?"

"And his brother."

Roman's brows crash instantly, and I jerk in his grasp, but he doesn't relent, his long fingers spreading wider for a better grip. A shadow falls over him, and slowly, he pulls in a lungful of air.

"We don't have to do this, you know?" His dark eyes implore mine. "I've been home for weeks now."

"And I've been eagerly awaiting your departure since the day you arrived."

"Lie to yourself some more, Kitten."

Kitten.

The nickname he gave me the day he met me. We were only fifteen, and he was too charming for his own good, so instead of feeding into his flirty ways, I snapped back.

He said he liked my claws, and that was that.

He became the boy I pretended annoyed me—until I didn't—and I was his 'Kitten.'

But that was twelve years ago, and not a damn thing is as it was then.

I swallow, working to keep my frown in place. "Do not call me that."

"That wasn't a denial." The asshole has the audacity to grin.

"Why are you here, Roman?"

"I work here. My name is on the building out front, right beside yours."

We stare at one another for a long stretch but knowing that was not what I meant, neither of us having to say it out loud.

Why did he come back? Why now?

Why at all?

I stand taller. "I'm running point on this, and I planned to do so with you on the opposite side of the country."

"In-person communication is always best."

"Communication?" A humorless laugh leaves me. That's rich. "And here I thought you were the radio silent type."

He jerks closer, eyes narrowing. "Want to take a trip down memory lane?"

I swallow my tongue, my muscles coiling in an instant, but I manage to force my words out strong.

"We've gotten this far without the added inconvenience of your presence. I don't want you here or tagging along. In fact, I would almost beg you to skip the weekend altogether, help avoid any... mishaps bound to walk in your wake. So, what do you say, hmm?" I tip my head, aware I'm acting like a brat and not giving two shits. "Hop on your fancy new jet and fly back to wherever it is you call home?"

"This is my home, Noel. I said I'm here to stay. I meant it."

"Yeah." My lips twist mockingly. "We'll see."

He regards me for a long moment. "A pessimist now, are we? What happened to the doe-eyed woman who fell in love with a story *from a magazine I bought her* that inspired all this hard work?" He shifts closer, bringing us face to face, his large fingers still wrapped around my bicep. "You were such a dreamer, a romantic."

"Aw." I reach up, straightening his tie. "Is your memory from before or *after* you packed up in the middle of the night and moved across the country?"

His body goes rigid, his eyes slicing to my ring finger—beautifully bare of the princess-cut diamond slid onto it five years ago.

My stomach grows queasy at the memory, but I paste on a saucy smile and pat his chest. "You may have brought me that magazine knowing I'd love the story inside it, but everything that came of it was because of my ideas." I glare. "And in case you were wondering, I despise the naive young woman who shared those ideas with the fickle young man with every fiber of my being."

What a fool I once was.

"If I didn't think you were capable of stealing the idea out from under me, as you not so subtly threatened to do—"

"I never threatened you," he interjects.

"No, you just forced my hand, refusing to allow me to rescind the contract that kept us tied together, but again, if I didn't think you were capable of screwing me over, I would have cut you out completely, contract be damned." Eyes hard and condemning, I pin them to his. "Have a shitty night, Mr. Dominion. See you in the air."

With that, I get the fuck out of there.

THE PERKS OF BEING CO-OWNER OF A MULTI-million-dollar company is avoiding the jungle that is an airport during the holidays. The downside is the dark-eyed, dark-haired, black-hearted other half of the equation, sitting right across from me and currently burning a hole in my cheek with his unwavering gaze as he waits for mine to meet his.

Roman Dominion, the six-foot-six walking, talking cologne commercial. You know, the kind where a mysterious man climbs from a sleek and sexy sports car, forever dapper in a freshly tailored suit. The ones where the man always has that slightly slicked hair he chooses the perfect moment to run his fingers through it, head tipping the slightest bit to really drive it home with that perfect shot of his sharp jawline and flawless lips, seconds before they hike into a dirty little smirk.

That's the thing about marketing, though, isn't it?

The prettiest of pictures are painted, creating an elusive image behind the screen, one never to be lived up to, but forever strived for, a couple thousand dollars at a time.

If only all women knew what I did, that the man behind the screen is nothing but a perfectly packaged façade. A hook, waiting to sink itself into the first fool to take the bait, but you know what happens when the fish gets caught on the line?

It's appraised, carefully considered, and if she doesn't impress, back in the water she goes... an ugly little scar left as a reminder.

As if she could forget.

Roman is literally a poster child for parents, the one where the fathers would say stay away from men like that, and the mothers? They'd doll you up and take you right to him.

"Careful, wouldn't want to give yourself wrinkles." Roman's words are teasing, but his tone deceives him. Too low. Too cautious. Completely giving him away.

It's killing him to be left to wonder what's on my mind when, once upon a time, he was the one I chose to share it with.

Oh, how quickly things can change.

I feel the scowl on my features before he points it out, but I keep it firmly in place as I pull my eyes from the expanse of gray clouds outside the small square window, pinning them to the man sitting in the heated, luxury white leather seat across from my own, nothing but a three-foot, retractable table separating us from one another.

His gaze flits across my face with swift movements, desperately searching for a sign of what I'm thinking, so I give him what he wants, removing the mask and revealing the stark truth of what I see when looking at him.

I stare at Roman, the self-made mogul of West Keys, who lives to buy, sell, and trade, and is damn good at it. The newly broadcasted billionaire—I knew I should have skipped that issue of *Cosmo*—who stands the tallest and most assured of any man in any room. Number one on *New York Times'* list of the year's most eligible bachelors. Successful, sexy, *single*, as printed in big, bold black letters beside his photo.

My academic rival through high school and college.

My business partner.

The man who loves thunder and warm whiskey.

And my biggest *fucking* regret.

Roman's features harden, creases forming along his forehead and deepening as his neck stretches, allowing him to keep his attention on my face as I push to my feet.

"Noel—"

"I'm going to say hello to the pilot. Consider yourself lucky if your feet ever touch the ground again."

Asshole.

CHAPTER 2

❄

N oel

"DINA!" I THROW MY HANDS AROUND MY SENIOR executive's—a.k.a. my favorite cousin—neck, hugging her. "Thank god for your fear of commitment."

Dina laughs loudly, squeezing me tightly before pulling back and hugging her tablet across her chest. "Literally, right? Who else would agree to trade their six-hundred-square-foot flat in the city for a five-story mega mansion turned resort, tucked deep in the mountains, blanketed in white and drowning in hot, slightly untamed snow-boarders?"

Humming, I accept the champagne Dina's assistant offers, spinning to peer at the upper-level lounge, the blue and silver garland elegantly braided along the railing gleaming in the light, and bringing a smile to my lips. "You will have to point me to where I can find me one of them."

"Oh, girl, they're everywhere. I can introduce you to—"

A throat clears behind me, and Dina whips around while I take the time to roll my eyes, downing my drink.

"Well, well." My cousin cocks her head, wild red curls falling into her face. "Look what the blizzard botched to bury."

My lips twitch, and I turn back around as Roman's hands slide into the pockets of his slacks.

"Nice to see you again, Dina." He dips his chin.

"Hm." She flicks her gaze along his form, pretending he's the least impressive being she's ever seen.

My cousin is a fiery woman, two years younger than my twenty-seven, and the person who not only convinced me to accept the job I'd secretly applied for and was offered but packed her shit and made the move to Los Angeles with me. That was nearly five years ago, and we haven't looked back since.

Facing me, her smile breaks free. "The bar was restocked to offer more budget-friendly items, as you insisted, and the new snow and ski gear you wanted for the shop is being unloaded as we speak. All rooms are ready to roll, thank-you cards and gift baskets left waiting in each invited guest's room, but I want you to review them, just in case, before everyone begins arriving tomorrow."

Her assistant hands me a checklist as if on cue, and I tuck it beneath my arm with a nod.

"How did the chefs do with the menu?"

"Freakishly delicious! Confirmed to be straight from the recipes provided and prepared to perfection. All staffed chefs took turns demonstrating each meal with little to no retraining required."

"And the upscale options?"

She purses her lips, and my shoulders fall.

"Dina."

"Seven."

"We went over this. Twice." I shake my head. "I said five max."

"I know, but the ideas are so good! They basically took items we didn't choose and turned them into ones we should have."

"No. You have to cut somewhere."

"And break their pretty little hearts?" she gasps dramatically.

"Oh, please—"

"I have an idea," Roman pipes up.

My attention snaps his way. "You're background music, remember? Numbers, contracts, and not much more than that."

"Let's allow the man and woman who inspired this place to taste test," he begins, ignoring the fact that I fed him the same line he did me when insisting we still take this leap together. "Have them decide what we keep. They would understand the food better than anyone, yes?"

"It's food."

"It's passion." His dark eyes flick to mine. "It's feeling and comfort and decadence. It's what all friends, couples, families will experience just before the night ends while reliving—or recovering—their moment of choice. It's the romance, and as you have said time and time again, *food* is a part of the foundation for these two."

My heart beats a little harder as I stare at the man I never should have wanted, but did, the thick, suffocating silence stretching between us. At least that's how it feels for me.

As if he knows, as if he senses the torment the simple sight of him creates, his sharp features soften into an expression I can't seem to forget, no matter how many times I've tried.

I turn away.

"That's actually a really good idea, Ells," Dina quietly agrees. "Their car is picking them up from the airport now. Maybe they'd appreciate lunch waiting for them in their suite when they arrive?"

"Fine. Set it up, but only if it won't delay their arrival for the opening ceremony." My voice is raspier than I'd have liked, and I refuse to meet either of their stares, already stepping in the opposite direction. "I'm going to find a few staff members in housekeeping, see if they have any last-minute concerns they might be too afraid to bring up with their boss."

"And you think they'll tell their boss's boss those concerns?"

I ignore Roman, counting the clicks of my heels as I walk away.

If I'm going to get through this weekend, I need to keep this man as far away from me as possible.

Should be easy enough.

He has been invading my office building back in LA for close to a month now. Why, I haven't worked out yet, but I've managed to only cross paths with him once or twice a week. Thankfully most of those being amid team meetings, where I purposefully placed him on the opposite side of the room. I'm also not *too* embarrassed to admit that I snuck out of my own company nearly every day, sometimes waiting until I knew with absolute certainty he was unable to spot me on my pitiful escape.

Melanie, my in-office assistant, who chooses to work as late as me most days, would text me to let me know he made his way to my floor and asked for me.

I've opened the parroted message from her twenty-three days in a row now.

The twenty-fourth would have been last night, but the persistent man caught me at my computer before I could run like a coward, pretending I was simply an extremely busy busi-nesswoman.

If he cared to ask around since his arrival, then he knows full well what a workaholic I've become and would have easily learned the first time my staff has witnessed my departure was the day he arrived... and every one thereafter. I was *always* the last to leave the office.

Pathetic to hide from him? Extremely.

Necessary to hide from him? Abso-fucking-lutely.

I spend the rest of the day being the final eye on all aspects of the event, nothing but simple, small changes that are more preference than anything else, like adding fairy lights to the dessert bar set up for the ceremony tonight and swapping out the red candles lining the mantel with blue ones to maintain the festive theme while also avoiding the clash of color from the flocked trees framing the fireplace.

Ultimately, this is a holiday retreat, but to appeal to all potential customers, we've locked onto the picture-perfect, snowy winter's dream.

"You look exquisite."

I've only gotten one foot out of my suite door when the familiar, silken voice weaves around me, clawing at my skin like the thorns of fresh-cut vines.

My eyes flash to his, my steps faltering as I swiftly yank my door closed behind me.

Roman has traded in his standard business attire, now dressed to kill in the purest of royal blues, his undershirt as black as his hair, deepening the depths of his midnight eyes.

A ghost of a smirk pulls at his lips, tugging at the threads knotted around the organ in my chest.

He comes closer. A single white rose in hand.

My stomach turns, the gesture a painful, familiar one I once adored.

He holds it out, and it takes everything in me to keep my hands clenched tightly around my clutch.

"Who do I have to fire?"

One dark brow rises, and it somehow makes him all the more striking.

"Who told you what I was wearing tonight?"

Roman's grin grows slow, and my god, his time away has done nothing to dull his bold beauty. If anything, it's amplified. His jaw sharper, shoulders powerfully set, proof he still takes his morning trips to the gym, rippling against the material of his tailored jacket.

I bet the Florida women just loved *this man.*

"Why the sour face?" He cocks his head.

My eyes narrow, and I go to step beyond him, but he blocks my path, sliding into my space with grace no man should possess.

"No one gave away your color of choice, but I

know you, Kitten. Red would be to stand out, white isn't your style, and black is basic."

His eyes fall to the sweep of my gown, a heart-shaped bodice pressed tightly against my chest, delicately curving around my forearms. The off-the-shoulder straps dip into a deep U-shape, my spine slightly on display, the blue nearly identical to his but sequined.

I sparkle from top to bottom, my black choker, as well as the cuff along my wrist and shoes, making it that much harder to believe his choice of a black dress shirt was as coincidental as the suit itself.

But he's both right *and* wrong. White was never an option. Red, however…

I'm saving that gem for tomorrow night. So blue it was.

The tip of the rose caresses my arm, and I blink back into reality, glaring at the satiny smooth flower as if *it's* the enemy and not the man who holds it.

"Accept it, Kitten. Please."

Taking the rose, I spin, sliding it through the 'Do Not Disturb' sign hanging on my room door, then push past him, but his legs are longer and built like a Viking's, stretching beyond my smaller strides to reach the elevator first.

The doors open moments later, and he sweeps an arm out.

Rolling my eyes, I step inside, hating being trapped in such a small space with the man who smells of pine and clean linen, of rain and snow.

Of before...

I swallow, avoiding the mirror-like doors before us, aware of the picture-perfect couple we look within them.

"Do me a favor and stay on your side of the room tonight. After the opening speech, I'm nothing but a guest of the resort, and I'd like to enjoy the evening."

"And being near me prevents that from happening?"

This time I do look forward, my eyes locking with his in the silvery reflection.

"Yes."

Creases fall over his forehead instantly, but thankfully before he has time to speak, the doors click open, laughter and loud chatter reaching us.

I smile wide at the sound and set out.

Six years of grinding comes to life tonight, and after it, I'll figure out what to do with my future.

One thing is for sure. After tonight, I no longer have any reason to correspond with Roman Dominion on a weekly basis.

The thought should bring me a sense of comfort.

Why doesn't it?

CHAPTER 3

N oel

I QUICKLY FINISH OFF MY SECOND GLASS OF champagne, a perfectly planned amount to start the night off, and check my lipstick using the camera app on my phone.

Dina winks at me from the corner as I make my way to the small stage in the conference room turned ballroom venue for the night.

This room alone was enough of a selling point for me when we began the hunt for the perfect location for our holiday getaway resort. Stretching nearly across the entire fourth level, the large floor-to-ceiling windows make up each wall, blanketing the room in the soft glow of the snow-covered mountains, the sun had set about an hour ago, their silhouettes now illuminated by bright dangling lights, some stretching beyond sight.

Dead center in the back wall are two giant glass doors with long, curving antlers for handles, leading to a balcony that overlooks the outdoor firepit area. Beside the hand-built stone pits is a forty-yard stretch of nothing but snow, surrounded by a three-foot fence—the perfect spot for families to sit and enjoy a hot coffee or a hot *toddy* while watching their littles play.

This is where our gourmet breakfast buffet will be set up each morning, and those who get here early enough will be welcomed by the wildlife just off the hillside.

It's exquisite and at the moment, full of potential investors interested in a piece of the action.

There is no doubt in my mind Roman and I will have a pile of offers to pick from once the weekend is over, and with double the luck, we'll be able to cut the bank out completely while affording us the opportunity to be picky, possibly even counteroffering to get exactly what we hope for in the end—someone who will leave us in full control of decisions, whom only requires a monthly check.

Would it be beyond incredible to find someone as passionate about what we've built here as us? Of course, but we both know that's not going to happen, so basically, we're after the opposite, someone who will leave the report and all it entails to us, simply watching for that monthly check to hit their bank accounts.

IF IT WERE UP TO ROMAN, I'D ALLOW HIM TO PAY off the largest loan with his new fortune, but that would only embed him deeper, giving him more.

I don't want him to have a larger part of this place.

I want him out of it, but I know him, and he'd never entertain the idea of my buying him out if it were even a possibility, if only to torture me with his presence some more.

I swallow, lightly clearing my throat.

As I step up, lifting the mic to my lips, the noise settles, and it's all eyes on me.

"Welcome, everyone." I pause, waving at my

event coordinator's daughters as they drop onto their bottoms in front of the stage.

"To say it's surreal to be standing in this room with you all right now is an understatement. This dream is seven years in the making, and tonight, on this beautiful estate, we experience it together, yet none of us quite the same..." I smile, and I'm met with several others across the room. "Because here at Blue Mountain Memories, it is you who decides what world, or should I say moment or *memory*, you'll fall into as you enter your suites. The resort and all it has to offer outside of your rooms is simply here to make sure the entirety of your getaway is as equally dazzling."

I hold my arm out, gesturing toward the windows surrounding us. On cue, the lights outside brighten to a nearly fluorescent color, shading the snowy mountain sides blue, the snow blower decisively arranged and kicked on in the next breath, creating the perfect fairy tale moment as snowflakes begin to fall.

The room cheers, the children gasping and rushing to press their noses to the glass as I use the reprieve to signal to Dina, who ushers our guests of honor forward.

"Many of you know this," I continue, regaining

their attention. "But for those of you who do not, allow me to share. The inspiration behind this resort and all it offers came from an article I read in a sports magazine one Saturday morning in my college dorm room. The story was about a man and woman and the journey their love took them on, and who better to explain what this truly means than the couple themselves?"

I look to the edge of the stage with a smile that couldn't possibly be wider. "Please, welcome to the stage Noah and Arianna Riley, and of course, little Lori and big brother Ian!"

The applause doubles as the family steps onto the stage, their son holding on to his mama's hand while their youngest, and the sweetest little girl, wraps her arms tight around her daddy's neck, trying to hide from the crowd.

Noah smiles, nodding his hello as Arianna moves closer, offering me a quick hug before taking her husband's side and the mic.

With a quick, shy look at her man, she brings the microphone to her mouth. "Hi, I'm Arianna, or Ari, as most people call me." She laughs nervously, and the crowd is already enamored by her with a single word. "We want to thank Noel for not only asking us to be a part of this weekend's opening celebration but also for making such a place possible." Ari glances my way before taking a small step forward and sharing her story with those in attendance.

"My freshman year of college, there was an accident that left me in a coma. When I woke up, I learned I had lost months' worth of memories…" Her voice grows thick, and as if having sensed the heightened emotions would come in that exact moment, her husband is already at her side, his palm pressed to her lower back in silent support. "Including falling in love with the man of my dreams."

Small gasps fill the room, and I hold in my smirk, Roman deciding to ignore my request of staying away and choosing that exact moment to join me on stage. He and I share a quick look, both of us thinking the same thing.

We knew this was meant-to-be magic.

I accept the champagne flute he offers but move my gaze back to the glowing woman with the mic.

"I had no idea if or when those memories would come back," Arianna continues, "and unbeknownst to me, they were. I had no idea how I learned at the time, but something in me led me to cook one day, and the meal I made was one of Noah's family recipes that before the accident, he had been... very patiently attempting to teach me how to cook. Guys, it didn't work."

Everyone shares a laugh.

"Seriously, he's still the resident chef in our house, I swear."

Licking her lips, she smiles. "Anyway, I'm going to leave you to wonder if I fell in love with him all over again, or if I remembered and simply fell harder, because this beautiful resort is about what came *after*."

After a brief pause, she continues. "It was near the holidays when I had my accident, so Noah and I had missed so many firsts, and I knew, without a doubt, he was meant to have all my lasts. But even knowing so, and knowing he was the man I would marry, it didn't settle the sting of all the time, all the moments, we lost."

Noah shifts his daughter to his other arm, placing a quick kiss to her forehead, before leaning over his wife to add to the story, "So my brilliant wife gave me something I never thought a person could give back, seeing as I couldn't find a way to give ours back to her when she needed them most." Ari gazes up at him, smiling when their son tugs on the hem of her dress. Noah faces the crowd once more. "She gave me the gift of memories."

Table after table, eye after eye, they all are transfixed on the family beside me, staring in awe and waiting for more insight, unaware the next part this man will share is the one they're going to salivate over the most.

Ari passes the mic to her man and their daughter sneaks a peek, tapping at it and jerking her hand back when it echoes across the room. Noah chuckles, dropping his chin against her head in reassurance before speaking to the crowd.

"My wife and I were supposed to be celebrating our first Valentine's Day, but when I walked inside the house, I would have sworn it was Christmas." His features soften at his words. "And then I went into the kitchen, and suddenly, it was New Year's, and then she led me to the back patio. It was much like this." He looks around the room, at the pretty ball gowns and men in suits, at the twinkling lights beyond the windows. "She recreated a night that was meant to be special to me, but without her, it meant very little. The incredible woman at my side not only gave me the memories we didn't get to make, but she reset one that was extremely painful for me, one that would sting at the thought alone.

But now..." He smiles down at the brunette woman, who looks at him like he's the air she needs to breathe. "Now when I think back to that night, all I feel is love and gratitude, and let me tell you, those were the last things I felt the first time that night in my life rolled around. She hit the reset button, and I'll forever be grateful for it and for her."

As if it just dawned on the crowd this instant, as if they didn't spend months reviewing and prepping for possible proposals, the dozens staring this way have gleams in their gazes, the conclusion in their minds the same. This place? It's the first of its kind.

Exclusive.

Lucrative.

Potential to impact someone's life if done right.

Everyone stands at once, clapping as the family of four huddle together, Noah lifting their son up and looping him around his back for a piggyback ride. As if he's done it a hundred times before, the little man, with hair as dark as his dad's and eyes to match, locks his little hands around his neck.

"Noel and her gracious assistant showed us many of the ideas they had for the rooms a while ago, and I can't wait for each of you to relive, reset, or reclaim the memory of your choosing." Noah tips his head in thanks, he and Arianna waving at the crowd as they begin to step back.

Just to the left of the stage, Dina catches my eye and then wiggles her brows, her phone screen lighting up already, pre-drafted proposals likely hitting our inbox.

"Well done, Kitten." Warm breath curls around my neck like a heat wave, subsequently drawing goose bumps to the surface. "They'll grovel on their knees for you now."

I look up into Roman's dark eyes.

Why haven't you done the same?

"Noah, Ari!"

A small shout from the crowd has me snapping my head forward, and I look to find a blonde woman with a tall, dark-haired man at her side. She smirks. "Before you go, care to share if the rumors are true? Did you really sign a new contract to stay in California yesterday, locking you in with the NFL's Tomahawks for four more seasons?"

Noah laughs, looking to his wife for the okay she must give, as he winks at her next, dips his head, and smirks as he says, "The owners can be quite convincing, so that would be a yes."

The woman throws her hands up in triumph and drops back in her chair as Noah passes me the mic, but to my surprise... and utter irritation, the *not to be seen, supposed to be freaking silent* man beside me has longer arms, reaching across me to grab it first.

"We want to thank the Riley family for allowing us a glimpse into their story, and more. Mrs. Riley spoke a little about the way food brought the two together, so I thought you may like to know, every menu item offered for both room service and in the Red Pepper Steak House upstairs are straight out of the recipe books his mother left for them, each as heavenly and comforting as the next," Roman adds as if he too has a mental checklist of what to be sure to share on this stage before we part and the resort officially opens.

Roman nods his chin slightly, and the Riley family takes their cue, stepping down to take their table with a smile. "Everyone, another round of applause for the Rileys."

As the crowd quiets, I shuffle a bit to the left, but Roman simply erases the distance. His free arm wraps around my lower back, tugging me to him.

I keep my smile in place while trying to

mentally come up with a way to dig my nails into his flesh without being overly obvious.

Before all these people, he and I look like a perfectly coordinated couple.

Roman gives me a little squeeze, and I grind my teeth to keep from frowning.

"Thank you for joining us this weekend and bringing your families and friends to share in the celebrations. As mentioned in the invitation, we won't disrupt the holiday with talk of business, but I must take a moment to acknowledge the hard work of the staff here at Blue Mountain Memories as well as those back in LA at R&N Industries, both teams led by my partner and the woman I admire most in this world, Noel Aarons."

Sure, that's how it is.

Let us pretend I'm not the woman he forced to remain his partner after shit hit the fan so he could play king of cruel punishment.

We both know I wanted him out of my life.

Just like we know he's the one who refused to allow it.

Buuut, since he's forcing my hand, I go ahead and turn my eyes to him, hoping he can read the anger in mine. At the very least, I *know* he can tell the difference between my real and fake smile, but the moment he speaks, his deep, rasped baritone wraps around my every limb, thawing me without permission.

"Noel, the work you've done is nothing short of extraordinary." He stares directly into my eyes, and I couldn't stop the moisture from building within mine if I tried. "And I am proud to be a part of this journey"—my chest feels like it's breaking open, bleeding out for all to see—"and honored to be the man you've chosen to marry."

Every muscle in my body freezes, coils, and fucking tears.

What. The. Fuck.

I can't breathe, can't fucking move.

He didn't just say that.

He did not just stand here in front of all these people and say what he said.

How dare you...

Roman's eyes flash, his chin dipping, and only when dozens and dozens of people applauding ring in my ears, do I realize we're silently staring at one other. So I pull on the resolve I do not fucking feel, and I force my hand to rise, lifting my drink as it's all I can manage.

My hand shakes as I pull it to my lips, and I

wrench my gaze away, knowing, without a doubt, his is still locked on me.

I inch forward, wrapping my fingers around the mic, and he allows me to take it when I was almost sure I'd have to tear it from his fingertips.

"Thank you, Mr. Dominion." My voice is slightly uneven, so I clear my throat and try again, a little too peppy, even to my own ears. "Okay!" I pivot, but his chest meets my back, and I falter once more. "Um, please, mingle, enjoy, and when you're ready to head to your memory or missed adventure, you'll find the room number and key codes in your email right…" I look at Dina, and she jerks her chin in acknowledgment, blindly clicking the golden button on the tablet, eyes wide on mine. Several low hums fill the air, phones vibrating and softly dinging across the room. "Now." I find it in me to chuckle, and others join in. "Cheers!"

The light over the stage is dimmed, and I thrust the mic into Roman's chest, hastily making my exit.

I'm forced to smile and chat with the guests in the first row of tables, but I make it quick, and then Dina is at my side, the two of us hustling toward the back exit.

"What the fuckety fuck?!" she hisses. "What was that?"

My body shakes. "*That* is the reason Roman Dominion came home. To trick everyone in attendance into thinking the beautiful love story that created this beautiful place was made reality by a happy fucking couple."

Stupid smart bastard.

Tears threaten to slip free, but I blink them away. "What are the chances his little stunt is publicized for… everyone back home to see?"

Dina's quiet a moment, and my eyes slide her way. "I mean, we only allowed the local news station in for the evening, but both reporters from the city arrived with all the other invitees."

Fuck. This is just perfect.

"I take it we're not headed for the upper-deck bar as planned?" she whispers.

"I need out of here, Dina."

"I'll have a car out front by the time we get there." She starts pushing buttons on her phone, and before we've even exited the elevator, her arm is looping with mine, her task done.

Out front, a chill runs up my spine, the bite of the cool winter's air whipping around us.

"If I may suggest, you should grab coats." The doorman gapes. "Maybe some boots."

"We'll be all right." We quickly slip into the waiting black sedan. "Take us to a local pub, somewhere with a room?"

While the man appears puzzled as to why we'd leave a resort in search of a motel with a bar, he doesn't comment, simply nodding instead. "I know just the place, miss. Real pretty, giant Christmas tree with presents and everything. The owner competed in the winter Olympics last year!"

"Yes. There." Dina nods, turning her smile on me. "We'll find some homegrown Snow Joes to keep us entertained."

"Perfect." I pull the pin out of my hair, letting the long, brown locks fall in curls around my shoulders. "Work is officially over."

I need a stiff drink.

Maybe two.

And dick.

Definitely dick.

ROMAN

SHE'S PISSED.

More than pissed, I'm sure, but a bold statement needed to be made, so I made it.

Noel Aarons is mine. She was five years ago, and she is now.

Between handshakes and introductions, I lost the woman wowing in blue. From table to table, man to woman, everyone in attendance, without a partner on their arms, stared after the perfectly poised brunette beauty.

The curvy, cutthroat businesswoman, who, in contrast, is warmhearted and built of benevolence.

The best of both worlds.

The ideal woman.

My woman, though she needs some convincing.

I see it when she looks at me, the pain I caused her, the hate she's held on to.

The love she can't let go of.

I imagine she's tried many times to do just that, but she knows what I know.

She was meant to be mine.

"So, what do you say, Dominion? Can I count on your good word?" Jim Furrow grins around his glass of gin, tugging his wife closer to his side when she, yet again, drifts closer to my shoulder.

"I look forward to reading over your proposal January second."

The man's eyes narrow slightly, but a smirk curves his lips, as if he's sure I'm speaking simply to please those around us. "Of course, son. Enjoy the lovely weekend with your fiancée."

I grin, internally wincing.

"Thank you, Mr. Furrow. I will. I hope your room is all you hope it to be." Dipping my head, I swivel around the room, lifting my hand and running it through my hair to avoid the eye of several others trying to claim my time, but I have none to spare.

It's the first night I've been in the same space as Noel, where there is no work to be done, and I won't waste it.

So off I go in hunt of the woman who escaped me a little over an hour ago.

To my surprise, she was nowhere to be found; I searched the very place I expected her to be, but I know her. There is no chance she's holed up in her room, not with that dress on.

Not after I pushed her over the edge in front of four-dozen headhunters.

No, the fierce, fiery brunette, with eyes like liquid smoke and lips made of the sweetest satin, escaped.

Time to hunt.

Ready or not, here I come, Kitten...

CHAPTER 4

❄

R oman

I'VE NEVER BEEN THE KIND OF MAN TO HIDE IN THE shadows. I like being up close and personal.

I like control.

So settling into the dusty, dark corner of a pub that may have very well been built—and run—by Vikings, is not ideal, but I can't exactly step up to the two women at the bar, so incredibly out of place in their ballroom gowns, and toss the one I came to find over my shoulder. To be fair, I *can,* but there's a good chance it won't bode well for my balls if I did.

Noel sits perched on a stool, Dina at her side... a half-dozen others circling them in, both men and woman, curious as to where they came from and how they ended up here, where everyone looks as if they just came fresh off the mountain after a day of snow sports. Some of the men are in nothing but their thermals and socks, all gear gone, probably after their third pitcher of lager.

I watch Noel closely, the slight flush of her cheeks and the way she covers her mouth as her head falls back with another bit of laughter, her delicate hand free of the gleaming diamond once weighing it down.

A sharp sting settles in my chest, and I decide not to rush right over to her when I know the moment her eyes meet mine, they'll grow bitter. The smile on her lips will twist with distaste, and after that, sadness will stare back at me, poorly hidden behind those amber eyes. Or maybe rage after what I did tonight, but still, beneath the anger will be something deeper. Something she can't control, which only frustrates her more because of that fact.

However, the more time that passes, the more her intentions for the night become clear.

Noel has something to prove, but not to anyone else.

To herself.

Sorry, Kitten, but I won't allow it...

The crowd has filtered back to their tables, Dina and Noel on their second glass since I've been here, now dancing their way through songs I've never heard before, but I can't listen to the lyrics anyway. Not when my focus is glued to the luscious woman in the center of the room.

The gown she's wearing creates an even deeper curve to her hips, her full figure delicately wrapped in the glitter and glam, making my mouth water.

She sways her body seductively, her long chocolate hair teasing at the edge of her peach-shaped ass, begging me to close my palm around it and squeeze. Bite.

Lick.

My cock jumps in my slacks, my chest rumbling when her head falls back, her slender neck bared as if inviting my lips to come out and play. I'd start at the very mid-point of her throat, kissing and nipping, sucking until her muscles clench.

I want her nails digging into my shoulder blades, want to feel the sweet fucking sting that'll come *right* before she does. A desperate plea for release, while also the exact opposite—a frantic attempt to hold off for one more second, to live in the in-between of absolute fucking bliss before succumbing to the pleasure of our finale. I want to watch her come as I do, at the same exact time.

I want no other woman as I want her. Never have.

Never fucking will.

If she won't have me, I'll simply die a single man.

And the suggestively single man wrapping his hands around a body that doesn't belong to him might die too…

My eyes narrow and I push off the wall, watching. Waiting.

What are you going to do, Kitten, let him paw what's mine or bring those claws out?

Noel smiles at the blond-haired man with snow coveralls hanging around his waist, her arms locking around his neck.

Too intimate, but I'll allow it… for now.

She says something, and he laughs, leaning in to whisper into her ear.

I press closer.

She nods her head.

I step from the shadow.

He takes Noel's hand and drags her off.

I fucking follow.

"What in the fresh *hell* are you—" Dina spots me, then looks from Noel's disappearing form to me, eyes widening. "Oh damn."

She goes to dart forward to warn her, I'm sure, but I pin her with a hard look, and she has the sense to recoil.

"Fine," she growls, stabbing her finger into my chest. "But fix her, don't shatter already broken pieces."

My jaw clenches, and I want to stand and argue my case, but now's not the time, so I nod, hustling away.

Rounding the corner into a short hallway, I find they've stopped in front of a room door. Noel pulls a key, an actual *key*, from her little purse and opens it up for the two to step inside. He does, and after a moment's hesitation, a few bounces of her leg, she straightens her spine and does the same.

I don't fucking think so...

NOEL

HOLY FUCKING SHIT, WHAT AM I DOING? I WONDER AS I click the door closed behind me.

The door that is suddenly thrown right back open, the frame filled with a dark-haired, dark-eyed dream.

No...

The man behind me, Joe or John or something of the like, shouts, "Hey, what the hell, man?" But promptly, *smartly* closes his mouth when Roman bares his teeth, looking like a fucking lion ready to rip the poor soul's throat out.

"What the hell are you doing here?!" I shriek. "Did you follow me?"

"Does it matter?" He gets in my face, my neck stretching slightly as my heels of choice are on the lower side tonight. "You are clearly about to make a mistake you can't take back."

"What makes you think I'd regret anything that

happened here tonight?" I hiss. "Who the hell are you to intervene?"

"I'm yours." He presses into me. "And you're mine," he says so simply, his chest hard and the perfect contrast against my soft body.

Always has been.

No! Shut up!

He continues, "And you'd regret it because he's not the man you want in your bed. I am."

My cheeks heat and I glare. "You have *no* idea what you're talking about, and I am *not* yours!"

"The hell I don't, and the hell you aren't." His hands wrench into my hair, tugging the slightest bit, and my treacherous body bows for him. "I *know* I'm the only man who can give you what you need."

"Uh," a third voice breaks in. "Should I... go?" the man I completely forgot about asks.

"No."

"Yes."

Roman and I glare at one another, his eyes reluctantly lifting over my head.

"Stick around much longer, and you'll be watching my tongue work."

I gasp, pressing against his ribs to free myself, but get nowhere. "You're un-fucking-believable!"

"And you are fighting the inevitable."

"Why are you doing this?" I vaguely register the door opening and closing. "*Why* did you stand up there and make a fool of me?"

"I didn't."

"You did! There were reporters, Roman! It's probably all over by now, and if it isn't, it will be by morning."

"Good."

I gape at him. "No! Not *good*." My hands dive into my hair, and I pace. "My dad is going to see that."

"You don't speak to your dad."

"So! Your mom will see it too, and your—"

"Brother," he all but growls.

I cut off, my chin dipping as I look at him through my lashes. "Yes."

His lip curls. "If you think I give two fucks what anyone has to say about us—"

"There is no us."

"You're wrong," he continues as if I didn't interrupt.

"And if you think just because you said it, that means it's real, you're a fucking psycho!"

"Only when it comes to you."

I bristle, fists balling. "I am not yours!"

"You have always been mine."

I jerk back, but he erases the distance I put between us with a single stride.

"Even when the world saw differently, you were mine."

"That's not—"

"Yes, it is." His forehead meets mine. "It's true. You know it. I know. And now *everyone* knows it. I gave you five years, Noel. I won't give you any longer."

"Get the fuck out of my room, Roman," I whisper.

"Your room is at *our* billion-dollar luxury resort six miles from this place."

"I hate you." My hand clutches at his bicep, planning to push him back, but my grip only seems to tighten. "You know that, right?"

"I know you wish you did, but know this, Kitten, no one could hate me more than I hate myself for allowing things to go so far." His thumb glides along my cheek, and my body decides it loves the feeling, pressing against the firm yet soft touch. Roman's chest rumbles, his other hand firm at my lower back. "Bab—"

"Get out." I swallow, cutting off the endearment I refuse to hear leaving his lips.

"You're telling me to leave, but you're the one holding on."

Undeterred, he buries his nose in my hair, gliding it down until his lips are tracing my ear.

"Let me show you how proud of you I am," he whispers. "Just for tonight, and you can hate me again tomorrow."

My body aches, my soul threatening to tear from its hiding place, desperate to reach for its missing link. But to give in to this man?

After all these years?

How can I?

"Please," he begs, our bodies seeming to sway. "Say yes." Pulling back to look me in the eyes, hunger and need heavy in his. "Give in for one night."

"I did that once," I breathe. "I gave in, and everything around me crumbled."

"Because the pieces were supposed to be mine from the start, and you know it. You want me. I want you." His thumb comes up, pressing onto my lower lip. "Please."

I can't explain why my lips open for him, desperate for his touch. His taste.

For him.

He presses more firmly, and my chin lowers,

the pad of his finger grazing along my teeth, my tongue pressing up, tasting, and then my lips close around him.

His eyes clench closed, forehead wrinkling. "Kitten... I dreamed of your little licks."

My chest heaves, and I swallow a whimper, need pulsing heavily through my veins.

"What's in it for you?"

"I get to be the person you need in this world, if only for one night." His answer is swift, unpracticed, and dare I say... honest.

The air in my lungs turns to dust, choking me, but I focus on the last part of his sentence, to hide the way the first affected me. "What makes you think I'd let you stay, that I wouldn't use you and spit you out?"

"Do it. Use me." His grip on me tightens. "Use me until there's nothing left."

His eyes darken, and my words leap into my throat before I can stop them.

"One condition."

Suspicion gleams in his gaze as he waits, preparing to argue should he not like what comes next, but it's simple, really. Necessary.

"Don't say anything else like that again."

He knows what I'm referring to. He doesn't like

it, doesn't like having the idea of holding back his need for me to *need* him, his desire to be the object of my desire.

He stares at me for a long moment, almost too long, but then my back hits the wall with a soft thud a second later. "Fine," he rumbles, making sure I know he's unhappy with my rule, but it ends with that one word.

His mouth crushes mine, and my sense of self-preservation dies a quick death.

Just like that, I'm at his mercy, his will.

I might just do anything he asked from nothing but the touch of his mouth on mine.

The man my dreams are made of.

The man who ruined my life.

Kissing him is everything I remember, yet it's light-years different from the first, last, and only time he took my mouth as his.

It's raw and hungry, desperate and needy. His tongue punishing and angry, demanding entrance as it sweeps, marking everything it touches as his and his alone.

My dress is hiked to my hips, and he yanks my leg up, hooking my ankle around his waist, my tongue fighting with his, but submitting when his lusciously long, *hard* cock grinds against my clit.

My hand sinks into his hair, tugging, and he growls.

"Fuck, yes." He tears away, dropping to his knees and draping my dress over his head as he perches my heel on his bent knee.

It's as if my pussy is the holy grail, and this is his one chance to touch it; the man wastes no time, his mouth hot on my center, over my panties.

He bites, and I cry out, my palms planting on the wall at my back, head thrown against it.

Warm fingers meet my inner thigh, slowly caressing the path along the stretch marks there until they're curling around the silk, tugging them aside.

"Fuck, I've dreamed of this." The heat of his tongue blankets my pussy.

He starts as far back as the position allows him to reach, lapping up and over my clit and pulling it between his teeth for harsh, powerful sucks.

He doesn't go easy, doesn't allow any lead-up, but I fight it, and his lips vibrate with a deep rumble.

"Give me what I earned, Kitten."

The man commands me to the edge and right over it.

I shiver, quake, and then I break, my hands

trying to find and grip his head, but he's covered by my gown.

I push against him, fighting him away, and his dark chuckles waft over my oversensitive clit, making my thighs clench all over again.

"No. One more," he warns, flying in again and sucking ruthlessly, two fingers slipping inside my pulsing pussy, and I clench around him, my body beginning to sag.

His hands come up to steady me, his grip firm on my hip, holding me to the wall.

"Another," I gasp.

"There she is," he speaks against me. "Fucking knew you'd open that pretty mouth for me. Keep telling me what you want, I'll give it to you, Kitten."

He slides a third digit inside me, and I sigh around the stretch, earning a groan from him.

I come quick, and suddenly, he's standing, holding me up with his body and the wall. He stares with hooded eyes, sliding his fingers into his mouth, sucking them clean with filthy lapping, slurping sounds.

"Tastes like mine." His mouth claims me once more, and he swivels us, masterfully unzipping my dress and easing it down my shoulders.

A hint of panic washes over me, and my eyes flash open. I reach out, flicking the light off, covering us in darkness.

Roman freezes instantly, and for a moment, neither of us moves.

And then the light's back on, and I'm met with a hard glare.

"I want them off."

"You said one condition. That wasn't it."

"I changed my mind." I lift my chin.

His face goes blank, completely unreadable, and he steps back, arms falling to his sides.

"Tell me why." His words are a demand but flat.

"Because I said."

"No." He shakes his head, grips my chin and holds it high. "I said... tell me... why."

And you know what? Fuck him...

ROMAN

I'M BARELY HOLDING ON TO MY SANITY HERE.

I've finally got the woman I love's flavor coating my tongue, her scent clawing up my nostrils, and she does this?

Hides from me, as if it won't be a fucking honor to see, touch, and taste every inch of her body? As if I didn't dream of this, of her, every fucking night for the last five years and many years before that?

Noel squares her shoulders, fire in her brown eyes. "God knows what kind of women you sleep with, but I'm sure all of them wear single-digit dress sizes."

My face falls, a sharp pain settling in my chest.

Baby...

Have I not made it clear how I see her?

Does she think my being away, somehow, magically means her curvaceous, buxom body isn't the same body I've always craved?

Me.

The man who has loved every fucking inch of her, always. Who wished to worship her curves, to tell her how beautiful and perfect and fucking sexy she is every goddamn time I have the chance?

It's never been about her body, which I love just as much. It's her.

She could gain a hundred pounds, lose a

hundred pounds, and as long as she is healthy and happy, I wouldn't care.

Why the fuck would I?

I love her. All of her.

But she's never allowed herself to let you show her how much...

My brows crash, my arms rising to the curve of her waist and gently turning her until her calves meet the mattress to our left.

"Okay, baby." I cup her cheeks. "If that's what you want, it's yours."

My voice betrays me, my internal agony seeping into my tone, and she picks up on it, a small frown building along her brow.

I reach out and shut the light off, shielding us in darkness. Pressing my knee into the mattress, I lower her onto it, my vision fighting for sight in the dim room as I bring my lips to hers.

"But just so you know, my sweet, stunning Noel... you're wrong."

Her lips part, ready to fight, but I don't give her the chance.

"There has been *no* other woman. There will only ever *be you*."

She sucks in a sharp breath at my admission, but I don't let the truth linger long.

I seal my mouth with hers, and while it takes her a moment, she responds, kissing me fiercely as she shoves my jacket from my shoulders.

I shrug out of it, grinding down into her, our teeth clinking, hands flinging everywhere they can reach, desperate to feel what we've missed out on all these years.

And it has been *years.*

I knew she was the one I wanted since high school, and while I fooled around over the years, I saved as much as I could for her and her alone because I knew our time would come. Especially after that night five years ago. I haven't so much as blinked at another woman since then.

Noel tears my belt from my pants and shoves them down.

I fall onto my back willingly, smirking as she swings a leg over, straddling me like her favorite stallion.

And then the light flicks on, and my eyes snap to hers, my groin on fucking fire, mind going haywire at the sight of the most beautiful woman I've ever seen hovered above me, her long brown hair spilling over her shoulder, her body ready to take my cock.

"Don't look so smug." She tries to hide the

small grin on her lips as she eases her dress down her shoulders, but doesn't drag it any farther, the smallest hint of nipple teasing where the material paused its descent.

"Oh, I'm feeling really fucking superior right now."

Her eyes flare. "Let's fix that."

She takes the belt and grips my hands, bounding the thick leather around my wrist, and tugs, shoving them above my head. Her eyes flash in warning not to move right as her full, soft tits pop free.

I groan, driving my hips up into her, but she lifts suddenly.

"This won't be sensual," she swears rapidly. "It won't be sweet or soft or some sort of cathartic moment. We fuck, we fall asleep, and we forget about it tomorrow."

I scoff, eyes closing as I grind into her again. "You're soaking through my pants. Free me. Let me in."

"Roman."

My eyes snap open, challenging.

I heard her, and I don't agree to the terms, so I wrap my hands around her body and thrust up into her, making her gasp at the feel of me before dipping one hand down to spring my dick.

"I hear you, beautiful. You want to strip me of years of longing so you don't have to admit you've felt it too."

She frowns, and I pretty much destroy my zipper, yanking myself free and giving the base a good squeeze before letting go and lifting her, aligning it with her entrance.

"You want to be fucked. You want to scream when you come, and you want to feel nothing but that biting bit of pleasure. You want to drip down my cock until I'm soaked in you, and you want—"

She drops down on my dick, those brown eyes wild and wanting, and we both moan on contact.

Me. You want me.

Noel doesn't play coy. Doesn't shy away.

She rocks, long and deep rolls of her hips, grinding her clit into me as I push her shoulders down, driving myself deeper into her heat.

Her gaze is locked on mine, holding as her back begins to bow, her mouth making a sexy little 'O' shape, so sweet, I can't resist slipping my thumb inside.

She moans, sucking around it, licking the tip of

my finger and taking it deeper as she clenches around me.

"You're thinking about my cock between your lips, aren't you?" I keep our pace, every fucking part of me fascinated by her. Dying to take her slow and steady, to fuck her so deep that I reach the block in her mind that keeps her from giving herself to me fully when I know she wants to. But I'll be what she needs before I take what I want. "I'll allow it, if you say please."

She cries out, her head falling back farther, forcing her to take her eyes from mine, and my finger pops from her lips. "If I got on my knees for you, you'd be the one begging."

"I wouldn't have to, Kitten." I drag my finger down, the cool of the leather still locked around my right wrist, drawing a shiver from her as I drag a trail of her saliva along her throat and chest, where I then grab her left breast, swiftly closing my lips around the rosy peak. "You've been dying to take me in your mouth, just as much as I've been dying to slide inside it. To watch you gag around me, but if you asked me to beg... know, I would."

I bite down and her pussy clamps down.

"Your walls are squeezing me, over and over." I

move to the other nipple, flicking it with my tongue. "Are you going to come already?"

"Mmm... yes."

I flip her over, pressing her knees high against her sides, and drive my cock back inside her.

She gasps, her back flying from the comforter as she digs her heels into the mattress. Lifting her hips into me. "God, yes. Deeper."

I pull out and she whines, her head snapping up, eyes frenzied and nearly black as she licks along her lower lip, watching me crawl down her body until my mouth hovers over her clit.

She begs with a second whine, hips seeking my salvation, but I only flick her with the tip of my tongue.

"Roman," she growls.

"Moan it," I tell her, lowering and sucking her lips into my mouth. "Moan my name."

Her gaze narrows, but her mouth parts, body shaking.

I close around her clit, rolling my tongue along it, and suck hard.

She jerks, nipples sharp like diamonds begging to be touched, so I give them what they want.

I'll give all of her whatever the fuck it wants.

With my free hand, I slowly glide two fingers

into her pussy, and she shakes, thighs clamping around my ears like pillows. I have to let go of her clit for a quick kiss, and I swear her eyes close at the feeling.

And then I start fucking her again, hands and tongue working her over.

"So good," she praises, fingers driving into my hair. "You feel so good."

Say it, baby. Say my name.

I press my thumb over her hole, and she cries out, holding my mouth where she wants it while pressing back into the pressure of my thumb, the tip earning the slightest entrance.

"I want to take you here." I lick around my thumb. "Tell me no one has?"

"Your cock. Please."

Almost...

"Fuck, I need to come. Please."

I curl my fingers inside her pussy, my motions swift, my tongue even faster.

"Roman," she whimpers, shaking and reaching for my arms. "I need you inside me. Now."

I've never moved so fast in my life, pinning her to the bed, her legs open for me, my cock finding its home without direction. I moan. "Baby, this pussy's swoll. Ready."

"Yes." Her eyes close. "So ready." Her fists wrap around the bars of the bed, bracing herself.

So I give her what she wants.

I fuck her senseless, the bed rattling, hitting the wall with quick, harsh thuds as I pound into her. Every muscle in my body coils, my thighs clenched to the point of pain, but I don't let up. I lift her hips, spread her wider, and dive in deeper.

She gasps, and I groan.

"There we go," I coo, sweat rolling down my back.

Noel begins to shake, her cries louder, short screams of ecstasy, over and over. Her hands leaving the post to squeeze her breasts.

She trembles as she roughly tugs at her nipples, her mouth clamping shut, a harsh whoosh pushing past her nostrils. "Fu-fuck." Her teeth are clenched. "My *god*, you're a fucking god."

Her heels meet my ass, and she pushes, willing me deeper, but I'm all the way in.

So I lean forward, giving her some of my weight, and she mews at the feeling.

And finally, fucking finally, her nails meet my skin.

"Dig 'em in, baby. Make me bleed for you, like

you'll bleed for me. I'm fucking you so deep, I know I've earned it."

"Choke me," she whimpers.

My eyes slice to hers, my cock swelling.

Hers open, meeting mine, hazed and dazed with ecstasy. "Choke me, Roman. Bite me."

I groan, my right palm flattening beside her head, my left squeezing her tit and yanking on her rosy peak just like she had. Her eyes flutter but don't close.

"Do it," she begs, eyes black with pleasure. "Do it, and I'll come all over your cock… and then I'll lick it clean."

My chest rumbles, my jaw twitching as I thrust fast and hard into her, her legs spread wide behind me, heels pointed at the sky as she pants beneath me.

She grips my left hand, drawing it to her throat, but I shake my head, grabbing the long, thick leather still latched around my wrist, and stretch it across her delicate throat.

It's cold against her hot skin, and she gasps, but her smile is downright sinful, her neck stretching, inviting me to do with it as I please. My hands make fists, sliding along the mattress and tightening against her.

She presses up into it even more, gasping for air she can't quite get, and I pull my cock back to the tip, slamming inside her. Again and again.

Noel's eyes roll back, every inch of her quaking. "So fu-fucking go-good."

She cries out, her body arching in unnatural places, and my cock hears her screams, feels her cream, and joins her.

My cum shoots from me with force, filling her cunt, and it doesn't seem to stop. I collapse onto her, my hips jerking, ass clenching, and she moans into my ear.

Just when I think we're done, she gives a little shove, and then I'm on my back.

And Noel does as promised, crawling lower to lick up my shaft, and my eyes threaten to close, but I keep them locked on the lips wrapping around my dick. My muscles clench, hand shooting out to touch her face, and her lids flutter closed, soft, possibly accidental moans filling her throat as she licks me clean of her. Of me.

Of us.

When my thumb grazes her bottom lip, slick with the cum she sucks free, her eyes pop open, meeting mine.

Slowly, she releases me, her words nothing but a whisper. "You earned it," she says as if to explain.

It's her way of *taking away* the intimacy of the moment, so I simply nod, and when I jerk my head toward her pillow, she crawls back up, lying down beside me.

I'd have grabbed her if I didn't think it would send her running.

It would have.

Then we lie there, staring up at the ceiling, nothing but our heavy breaths filling the air around us.

I know this was a physical act, a deep-rooted, long delayed need for one another finally coming to the hilt, but it was so much more than that too.

There's a part of me that's clawed at my insides for years, constantly fighting for air it could never quite find, an ache down in my bones. It lessened a little that first day I walked into her office in LA, and for the first time in years, met those deep brown eyes, shock and a whole lot more swimming in them.

The pain is one I've carried with me every day the last five years, but right now, this very second I'm searching for it, the lax, calmness I've fallen into so foreign it nearly draws me to tension itself.

I know I'm not the only one, as the woman beside me's eyes have fallen closed, a soft, serene smile on her perfectly plump lips.

I'm not fool enough to assume she'll wake with the same lapse of self-control. She won't.

Tonight, this was—no.

I was her moment of weakness. She allowed her body to make the call her mind won't entertain, and what her body needed, what it craved, was my touch. She fell headfirst into years of repressed desire.

Tomorrow she'll try and place her wall back up, but what she doesn't know is that wall didn't simply lower itself for me tonight. It cracked and then crumbled into a hundred tiny pieces around our feet.

There is no rebuilding, and if I do this right, if I have my way, she'll realize she doesn't need it.

Not when it comes to me.

Not to protect her from us.

Tomorrow morning, she will pull away.

But I'll do all I can to draw her right back.

CHAPTER 5

N oel

WITH THE MORNING SUN COMES THE INEVITABLE sense of regret, but where I imagined it would dig beneath my skin, clawing at me to the point of pain, it's not. It's a softer sort of sting, like the ache between my legs, like my nonexistent abs—every time I move, I'm reminded of last night from every point of my body.

A small smile tugs at my lips because even regret and expertly earned body aches aren't enough to dampen the mood.

My plate is stuffed high with brown sugar pancakes, and my cappuccino is heavenly. The perfect balance and temperature for my taste. I'm sitting in one of the bistros set right at the corner's edge of the long glass railing, overlooking the snowy mountain morning, a fresh blanket of powder having come in overnight, covering the trees from top to bottom with hints of snowflakes in the air if you really pay attention. The sound of children laughing below and the subtle hint of holiday music whisper in the background.

There couldn't be a more enchanting sight to wake to and look out at than this, and not only the guests we invited get to enjoy it, but as of this morning, it's open to all, and from what I've heard, the entire third floor is now occupied, along with the first and second.

I imagine the look on the guests' faces when they walk into their memory of choice, be it the ultimate holiday getaway or their first trip to the beach, Halloween in December, or any of the other three-dozen memories we've created here.

I spent some time people-watching during my first cup of coffee, trying to guess if they came to relive a moment or experience something they may have missed for the first time.

So yeah, it's been a serene morning, and I'll admit, sneaking out and leaving Roman to wake up in the motel bed alone was the perfect way to start it. Satisfying even.

He was oh-so satisfying...

Chuckling at myself, I shake my head. "Get a grip, girl."

Bringing my coffee to my lips, I inhale the sweet, creamy beverage before taking a small sip and allowing it to warm my throat.

"Noel?"

My eyes pop open, and I peek to my right. "Arianna, hi." I smile.

"Oh good, it is you." The gorgeous brunette laughs as she walks closer, but stops after a few steps. "I'm sorry, I don't want to bother you, you, you look so comfortable."

My grin broadens, and I lean forward, setting my cup down as I wave her closer. "Please, bother me. I don't mind."

She grins, and I reach out, helping her lower her tray of muffins and pancakes onto my table before she eases into the seat across from me. "Hi."

Laughing, I tug my sleeves over my hands, sweats and matching hoodie the outfit of choice this morning. "Hi. I was hoping you guys would venture out into the hotel a bit. I imagine it's rough when everyone's always drooling over your husband."

Chuckling, she peeks over her shoulder. "Thankfully, he's not a movie star and isn't always recognized, so we've been exploring all morning. They're right down there actually, playing in the snow."

She shifts her seat some, and I stretch my neck to see a little farther, right as a teeny tiny little thing runs into view, black curls bouncing around her shoulders as she chases after her big brother.

"So cute. How old again?"

"Three and two going on ten, plus spitting images of their dad." She chuckles, a soft smile tugging at her lips as she looks at the tray of goodies. "And equally as obsessed with his pancake recipe as I am, Noah's already been up here twice, so I volunteered this round. Lolo literally eats them like chips. If you try and cut it up, she'll give her dad big pouty eyes, and he's got a new one for her in seconds. The sucker."

We share a laugh.

I decide it's safe to grab my coffee again, cupping the warm mug in my palms. "Yeah, I can't tell you how many times someone tried to talk me out of the all-inclusive breakfast buffet, but that was nonnegotiable. It's a huge selling point and the best way to bring everyone together before families split ways for tubing or boarding, or my fave, shopping."

Arianna smiles, tucking her hair behind her ear as she leans closer. "This place is seriously beyond anything we ever expected, Noel. Truly."

A knot forms in my throat, and I nod my gratitude, unable to speak the words, the praise from her so overwhelming I can't simply snap right out of the compliment.

She's the woman, the very essence of everything Blue Mountain Memories. To know she's blown away makes me want to bawl and dance and bawl some more.

"So, um…" She rubs her palms on her leggings. "I know it's not my place, and I know you're trying to enjoy your morning, but—Mr. Dominion!"

My muscles freeze and I slowly lower my feet to the ground, shifting just slightly to peek at him out of the corner of my eye.

My mouth waters instantly.

It's been a long, long time since I've seen the man in anything but a suit, and he looks absolutely divine in nothing but a pair of red track pants and a solidly fitting, white long-sleeve.

I'd bet he looked like a deity in nothing at all, but I didn't allow myself to indulge, though I felt the deep cuts of his stomach and the tight coil of his muscular arms as they braced at my sides.

Heat spreads in my stomach, and I swallow.

"Good morning, ladies." His eyes find mine, searching, narrowing in on the crimson creeping up my cheeks as I swiftly look away.

A hidden smile tugs at his lips, but he hides it behind the mug in his hands and joins us without invitation. His body purposely brushes mine as he squeezes by, leaning a hip against the corner of the glass as he looks out at the children playing below. "It's beautiful out here, isn't it?"

"It is, and actually… this couldn't be any more perfect." Arianna smiles shyly, looking between the two of us. "I would prefer if my husband was with me, but being as I don't know if I'll get another minute with you both this weekend…" She trails off, rubbing her lips together. "I was told you didn't want to talk business while here, and I thought that was really cool, but in the off chance someone gets to you before you're back in the office, can I steal two minutes?"

Anxiousness wraps around me, and my eyes fly up to Roman's as his palm subtly meets my back. My attention returns to Arianna. "Yeah, of course." I do my best to smile. "Is everything okay?"

"Oh!" She frowns, realizing my unease. "No, yeah. It's perfect, and that's sort of it." She looks between us. "This place is literally *perfect*. Noah and I didn't really know what to expect when you asked for permission to use our story as inspiration for your project. We were more than honored you wanted to create something like this, but we had *no* idea what you would turn it into. I mean, the tiny details in the room we picked and how you incorporated us into it without knowing which we'd choose. We... never expected that."

My features soften as it dawns on me. "You chose the preschool room."

It's not a question, her wistful expression says it all, her eyes glossing over as a gentle smile forms on her lips as she shares, "When my son was born, we got him the same little plush football Noah had made after my accident, so when he ran up and showed us the exact one from the chest of toys in the room, I..." She swallows, a brighter smile forming, this one reaching her eyes. "He was so happy he wouldn't have to share his with Lori for the weekend."

Both of us chuckle, allowing a moment of silence between us.

"Thank you," I speak softly, trying to calm my nerves waiting for the but.

"I don't know if you're aware, but our entire family joined us this morning. The second they checked in, we toured all their rooms, and everyone purposely chose a different memory or theme, and oh, my gosh!" She laughs. "Mind blown."

Roman squeezes my shoulder right as my exhale leaves me, and I smile wide at the woman before me. "That means more than you know, coming from you."

She beams. "I don't want to take up any more of your time; plus, I hear my son down there causing havoc, so I should probably go, but before I do…" She trails off, taking a deep breath and glancing over the railing at her family once more before looking back to me. "Noah and I would like to offer every penny you're looking for from investors."

My eyes bulge, my lungs refusing me air. "I… what?"

"We'd also like to pay off any loans that got you to this point."

"Arianna…"

She giggles at my struck expression. "We feel the passion, and we want to be a part of it. I think together, us simply silent support but equally passionate and dedicated, this place would have the best chance of staying exactly what you've created it to be, a literal dream vacation spot. I know how much it means to you, and we want to be a part of making sure it stays that way. When there's this much love put into something and coming from two people who clearly love each other just as much, it's going to be incredible."

A wall slams over me, my face falling, every ounce of happiness she poured over me mixing and diluting itself with guilt.

"Oh. Um… Ariana, we're… I mean, this…"

My gaze finds Roman's steady one, too many emotions swirling in his gaze for me to name. A frown builds across my forehead.

"You don't have to answer me now," she rushes as she stands, and my head snaps her way. "I just wanted to throw it out there and add we are literally ready to sign the check over to you now, and nothing is going to change our minds. I'll just be waiting and hoping for a phone call without the expectation of one. Well, that, and I wouldn't mind an invitation to the wedding."

I simply offer a close-lipped smile, shocked and confused, and everything in between.

"Enjoy your morning," she says. "You guys deserve it. Maybe we'll see you at the Christmas Eve feast tonight. Ian and his cousins are so excited to see 'Santa.'" She beams, grabs her tray, and walks off. "And if you need someone to make a playlist for the big day, I'm your girl!" She laughs, waves, and walks away.

"...bye," I say a moment later, but I'm not sure it came out as more than a whisper.

I stare out at the snowy hillside, the voices around me muffling until I hear nothing but my own thoughts, and I can't even make out any of the hundreds of things running through my head.

Roman lowers into the seat Arianna vacated and leans forward, his elbows perched on his knees.

He and I stare at each other a moment, and I drag my fluffy sock-covered feet back into the cushion, my free hand wrapping tightly around me as the other tucks my cup into my chest.

"Kitten—"

"Stop." I shake my head. "Just... stop. You knew, didn't you? It's why you came home after five years of staying away. It's the reason you've been showing your face around the office, why you came up on the stage with me yesterday, why you wore a matching fucking outfit and said I'm your future wife?" My nostrils flare in an attempt to keep from crying. "Because you knew what we were building here and what people would assume because of that, what people would want and what would sell more."

His brows crash. "That is not fair."

"Don't talk to me about fair," I hiss, torment seeping into my every word and exposing me to the man before me. "God." I look away. "What am I supposed to do? Sit around and lie? Let her think we're this love-struck couple who created a dream out of this completely selfless and utterly magical moment that she gave to the man she *did* love, who loved her back and never gave up on her and wouldn't *dare* walk away?"

"Noel, please," he murmurs somberly. "Can we have a real conversation? Please?"

I swallow, my brows drawn in tight as I finally whisper, "I don't know if you deserve one yet."

I don't know if I do.

81

Swiping a stray tear, from sadness or frustration, I don't know, I glance at the gondola in the distance to avoid his probing gaze.

"Okay," he says quietly, and I see him nod in my peripheral. "We don't have to think about any of that right now."

A scoffed laugh leaves me. "You stood up on a stage in front of everyone we work with and everyone we've ever considered working with and told them I was your fiancée, Roman. It can't exactly be ignored like everything else between us has been." I close my eyes. "And I just sat here and didn't correct Arianna freaking Riley, the goddess of all wives. The woman who built a damn library for a hundred schools across the country, who saved music programs in ten counties this year alone. And just last week, they sponsored an entire high school's football team, so they could afford to travel for the championship game they earned the right to play in but almost had to forfeit because of money."

"The woman who trusted this idea to you with zero knowledge of me."

I ignore his comment. "She's pure and honest, and I just… lied."

"You didn't lie, Noel."

My glare swings his way, but a smile pulls at his lips.

I stare at him, and this time, I allow myself to really look at him.

The sun shines along the left side of his face, highlighting the stubborn set of his jaw, but the harsh lines near his eyes are gone, the ones that appear when his stern features assess you, trying to dig their way deep into your core, but only to bury themselves so you can't claw them out.

His granitelike face has softened some, a newfound peace lightening the shade of his eyes, and I won't pretend I don't know the reason for it.

"You followed me last night."

His gaze holds mine for a moment. "No. You were quick, Kitten, but I found you."

"And interrupted my night."

He lifts a dark brow, and I will my cheeks not to pinken.

"That I'm not sorry for, and I would do it again in a heartbeat." He leans back, swirling what's left of his coffee. "So don't get any ideas later."

A huff leaves me, and I shake my head, but for some reason, a slight smile tugs at the corner of my lips. "You are absolutely ridiculous, you know that?"

I look at him out of the corner of my eye, and my *god*, the smirk!

"I don't see any whipped cream on that," I say quietly.

His eyes come up to mine, tenderness falling over him, creating an ache in my chest.

"Never could quite bring myself to add it anymore," he admits.

That tiny detail into his life shouldn't make me grin, but it does, and I drop my head back to look at the sky. "Damn it, Roman. I'm so angry with you." Angry with myself. "I used to sit around and make up conversations in my head, planning out exactly what I wanted to say to you, but now... I don't even know where to start. I'm just... so tired of hating you. It's exhausting."

"What if we didn't say a whole lot this weekend?"

Surprised by his suggestion, I glance at him as if to say 'go on.'

"What if we simply exist while we're here? What if..." He pauses, sliding to the edge of the seat. "You're my date to dinner tonight, and not for appearances, but because you want to be." When I don't immediately deny him, he continues, "What if you allow me the pleasure of sharing a bottle of wine with you later?"

"I won't allow you in my bed again tonight."

"If you remember right," he teases, cocking his head. "You didn't quite want me in your bed last night."

A laugh bubbles out of me before I realize it's coming, and my lips squash to one side in a small smile. "Five years, and not much has changed."

"The way I feel about you has never changed, Kitten, so if the Rileys were to ask me how dedicated and in love I am with this place, as well as the woman who made it happen, there would be no lies leaving my lips."

Moisture builds in my eyes, my throat running dry.

"Be my fiancée this weekend, Noel."

I swallow, my heart and brain on completely different pages. "And after it?"

"You get to decide."

"Decide *what* exactly?"

There's an innate strength to his face, a sheen of sureness brightening his gaze. "If you want to keep me."

"And if I don't, will you leave again?" I don't know why I ask this. I'm not sure I'd believe his answer either way, but I have a feeling I know which one he'll give.

Roman simply shakes his head, grabbing both our mugs as he bends beside me.

He presses a single, lasting kiss to my temple, and I close my eyes, willing myself not to get caught up in the man who said he loved me but left me, knowing I never untethered myself from him in the first place.

I should demand a conversation. I should have done that years ago, but I've never been brave enough to have it. I didn't want to know why he picked up and left instead of staying and fighting for what he claimed he wanted, even if that meant fighting me. After a while, I found a way to stop worrying about it and did what I needed to do.

I busted my ass, worked fifteen to twenty hours a day sometimes, to the point of exhaustion, and it paid off big time. How I could manage a relationship during that, I don't know, but I didn't allow myself time to wallow or wonder.

The truth is, I don't know if I'd change a thing if it wasn't guaranteed I'd land right here, right now.

Roman returns quickly, handing me my freshly made cappuccino and another latte for himself.

He moves his chair beside mine and gazes out at the ski lift ahead, so I do the same.

A moment later, a low, satisfied sigh leaves him, and I feel it in my soul.

I blink back the tears I don't quite understand and don't comment on the solid squirt of whipped cream spun high out of his cup.

My muscles seem to ease on their own accord, the heat of his body warming mine.

But, in the back of my mind, a nagging little voice warns me that it's a mistake to allow this, so why does it feel like making him leave would be a bigger one?

CHAPTER 6

R oman

I'M OUT THE DOOR BEFORE I'VE GOT MY LEFT SLEEVE rolled up, so I use the reflection in the elevator to make sure they're even. Just as the doors open on the bottom floor, the one across from mine does as well, and Noel steps out, her hair slicked back and pulled up into a high ponytail, thick, sleek straight hair still reaching her midback.

My teeth sink into my lower lip, thoughts of wrapping it tightly around my wrist and the sounds she'd make as I did it, looping through my mind.

A knowing smirk whispers along her plump lips, painted a soft, mauve color this time.

My eyes drop to the dress.

My god, the fucking dress.

Blood red and mermaid-shaped, the top wrapped around her throat, creating an ache in my fingers, dying to take the material's place now that I know she likes it.

Craves it.

She lifts a brow as the sight of me slowly begins to disappear.

"Oh shit." I thrust a hand out, stopping the elevator doors from closing me back inside.

Her husky chuckle reaches me, her almond-shaped cat eyes blinking slowly and coated in a thick, *naughty*, layer of black liner tonight.

She allows herself to look me over, zero hesitation as she loops her arm through the one I offer her. "All black. Interesting."

We reach the entrance to Red Pepper Steak House, and I lean closer, whispering into her ear, "What's interesting is you chose to wear your hair up, knowing good and well my marks are showing on your skin." My knuckles glide along the base of her neck and down her spine, caressing the places I kissed last night.

She lifts her chin, so I lower my ear to her lips. "As a good woman would if trying to please her man, yes?"

My chest rumbles, and she pulls back, eyes dancing with humor, but she quickly faces forward.

"Manuel." She beams, and I want to yank back the hand she offers him. "The place looks gorgeous."

The man bows his head with a smile. "Thank you for trusting my team to set up for tonight's event, Ms. Aarons. I think you and your fiancé will find your place near the fire to be the perfect place to spend Christmas Eve."

She stiffens, but keeps her smile intact, though grateful, I'm sure, for the moment the gentleman's attention shifts to me. "Mr. Dominion."

"Great to see you again, Manuel."

"Please"—he holds a hand out—"allow Katie to lead you to your table."

My palm finds her lower back, and we walk into the room as one. She pretends not to notice the way those around blatantly stare at her, and my chest puffs out with pride.

To them, the beautiful woman on my arm is all mine.

But as she lowers into her seat, the pride is gone, leaving behind a bitter tang in my mouth, as the only person who matters does not agree.

Confusion draws creases along Noel's brows, but as I look around the table, the same feeling settles over me.

I planned to take the seat opposite her. That way, she was in my direct line of sight, the center of my attention, but the table reserved for two is set for four.

"Expecting company?"

I had clung to the idea of having her to myself, of a night out together, just the two of us, like we've done a thousand times, but have been deprived of these last five years.

I settle into the seat at her side, and she grins, nodding her thanks at the waiter as he fills two wine glasses before silently slipping away.

"Disappointed?" she teases, her delicate fingers wrapping around the stem of her glass.

"Yes."

Her eyes widen, but quickly glitter with humor, and she shifts in her seat, angling her crossed legs toward me.

The urge to run my palm from her knee to her thigh, up under the slit there, is heavy, and the moment of pause that follows tells me she knows it.

She swallows. "We said no work, so we'll call this dinner a celebration."

"Of?"

"I'm taking the Rileys' offer," she rushes, her expression hardening, daring me to challenge.

Instead, I blindly reach for my wine, lifting it to softly clink against hers.

"You're not going to argue?" she says slowly. "Demand to review the offer and terms and write up your own in return?"

"Not today."

"I won't allow you to block this," she promises. "Due diligence will be done, but this is—"

"An unfathomed outcome? A best-case scenario?" I reach out, brushing my knuckles along her cheek. "A dream you never dared to dream come true? I know what that offer means to you, and I knew the moment it was given, our answer would be yes."

She sighs, her brown eyes luminous, her smile bright and beaming, pleased by my understanding and appreciation of the outcome.

"I missed this smile." My thumb brushes the corner of her mouth, and as I knew it would when the words escaped, it grows taut.

A wistful cloud covers her, her happiness tainted by our broken bond, her heartbeat calling out to mine, begging me to heal its torn pieces, but her mind contradicting the notion in an effort to shield her from it shattering all over again.

"I've missed you, Kitten. So fucking much," I murmur, pain lacing my every word.

A harsh breath whooshes from her, her eyes flitting between mine as I inch closer, allowing her enough time to pull away, hoping like hell she won't.

My lips meet hers, and her eyes close.

Fuck yes...

Longing whirls in my stomach, my free hand finding her outer thigh, but before the kiss can begin, she whispers against my lips.

"I think that's enough of a show." Her tone is thick and pensive.

My eyes flick open, narrowing.

"I would say you have them convinced."

My frown begins to deepen, but I don't have to ask what she means. My gaze then pulled to the couple weaving their way toward us.

Noah and Arianna Riley turn heads in hunter green, their expression brightening with each step taken toward us.

Noel clears her throat, speaking with her mouth hidden behind her glass. "I hope you know how a man engaged is supposed to act."

"I remember how a man in love *feels*."

Her head snaps toward me, gaze searching, but this time, I give her nothing, holding her attention as I push to my feet and greet our guests as they reach us.

"Mr. and Mrs. Riley." I smile. "Thank you for joining my wife and me for dinner tonight."

Noel stiffens at my side, and Arianna Riley?

She squeals.

I turn my smirk at the woman beside me, and my sweet, bratty Noel might as well be ravaging me right here for all to see as that is the face she's painted on, too damn good at masking her fury. I know she wants to gouge my eyes out, but to everyone else, she looks like a woman hungry for her man.

Me.

We pass pleasantries, listening to the couple's stories about their afternoon, but when the waiter comes back for a second time, and no one has taken the time to look at the menu, the conversation dies down as our guests take quick looks at the drink menu, so I use the moment to speak into Noel's ear.

"Better keep that mask on, sweetheart. That way, when the dinner is over, and your night becomes mine, you can pretend the need you have for me is fake too."

"You're going to pay for this," she warns.

"Why do you think there's a tie around my neck tonight, Kitten?" I nip at her earlobe discreetly, my low moan purposeful. "So you can knot it around your neck while I fuck you raw... just the way you like."

"Was I not clear?" she hisses, but squirms in her seat. "You're delusional if you think you're coming to my bed again tonight."

"That's okay, baby. I'll make sure you *come* in mine. Several times..."

Her nails dig into my thigh in warning, but my cock swells from the sting, bobbing up to say hello to her pinkie.

Her hand flies from my leg so fast I have to stifle a laugh, reveling in the shiver that runs down her spine. I torture her some more by stretching across the front of her for the menu, allowing my elbow to graze her sharp nipples, the dress not the kind to allow for a bra.

I meet her eyes. "Your pussy *is* mine." I pause, only adding the next word for her benefit. "Tonight."

Her thighs clamp together, and I sit back, throwing my arm around her chair, and tease her skin with the pads of my fingers. Right then, the happy couple across from us looks up, and we smile in sync.

Now, if 'tonight' could hurry up and arrive.

OTHER THAN A QUICK, TWO-MINUTE, 'WE'RE SO honored you want to be a part of this' and 'we can set up a meeting with our legal teams next week to go over the logistics,' the dinner was not ruined with talk of business.

Noah shared with us some of his experiences as an NFL receiver, and admitted he sometimes misses the quarterback position, while his lovely wife let it slip that baby number three is on the way, though no public announcements are planned to be made. Of course, we agreed to keep their little secret.

They were about to hand us complete control over our dreams with a giant check to go with it.

But after the accidental reveal of their growing family, Arianna asked about ours, and with each word Noel forced herself to speak, my heart tore a little more, because while the two at our table couldn't see through the mask, I could.

Complete and utter sorrow dug deep into the woman I love's words, pouring salt into the wounds I've yet to have the chance to try and heal. It shadowed her eyes and claimed the color from her cheeks.

To them, she likely appeared passionate and resound, but for the first time, I saw in her the result of my actions, felt the ample iciness she slew me in.

I know the thoughts that crossed her mind as she lied, shamed that there was technically no lie to speak of.

She did want children.

She did want a house in the country, to settle a world away from big city working life.

She wanted to build a home, much like the man

and woman who inspired us to reach beyond what we thought possible.

Had things been different, we might be halfway there by now.

Yet, there we sat, suddenly solemn, all hints of playfulness from the start of the evening gone, as we pretended to be together, but it was only the label that was a lie.

Because make no mistake, I love her with all I am, and Noel Aarons loves me to her core.

The problem?

She has all the reasons to hate me just as much.

This is exactly why I 'accidentally' knocked my glass over at dinner and allowed it to soil my slacks, so as we parted ways after eating, I could excuse myself to my room, giving Noel the space I know she needed and the time to swaddle her agony into anger.

Not to mention the forty-five-minute span she most definitely, filled with a few more glasses of merlot.

It doesn't take long to locate her, her infectious laughter falling over me before I can round the entrance to the fifth floor. I admire the large wooden beams above on my approach, stretching from one corner of the room to the next, long white wisterias hanging from the tops of it, silver and blue lights woven within them, creating a serene setting in the large area and holding it as you cross over into the open pub, the one and only place within the resort dedicated for the twenty-one and older crowd. It's not too busy at the moment, most of the guests having chosen to attend the event in Santa's Workshop tonight over this place, or at least as a starting point of the night.

As the night goes on, though, I would wager many couples will make their way here. The music is soft, the lights low, but the chatter is alive, and the glow is coming from the left corner of the bar, where the brown-haired beauty has situated herself.

I drop into a seat at the opposite end of the bar, my eyes roaming the room, taking in the subtle hints of Christmas plaited all around. Bundles of pine cones sit atop the tall beams of each corner, glittered layers of faux snow and poinsettias delicately mixed. Silver and red ornaments fill long glass vases and sit every few feet along the upper beams, mistletoe hanging over the edges with pine-colored ribbons.

A long sigh leaves me, and I spin in my chair, a

glass set before me in that exact moment.

My head pops up in question and the bartender nods his chin.

"Warm whiskey." And then he's gone.

I frown, my eyes snapping to the woman I came here to see.

Noel laughs at something one of her team members says as she raises her glass to her lips. Only then do her eyes slide this way.

They meet mine for a single second, and then they're gone.

My lips twitch, but the tension in my stomach doubles, tightening until I'm forced to sit taller. I down the glass in one go, tapping it on the bar top in signal for a second, which is passed my way quickly.

I won't throw this one back, though. No, I'll sip it slow, savor the bitter vanilla flavor as it burns against my throat.

This is her sneak attack, her silent little threat wrapped in a sugary surprise.

Noel is here for a good time, and I'm not to dare ruin it for her.

Guilt weighs heavy on my shoulders, as it should, and I have no intention of dimming her spirits that were on the highest high when the evening started, and judging by the looks of it—and the gesture—she's found a way to push the heavy aside and has gone back to relishing in her accomplishment.

She didn't have to acknowledge my presence, but she did, and with a warm memory, as small and insignificant as it might seem. My simple drink of choice, making sure I knew who it came from and inviting me into the celebration, if even only from afar.

This dream was years in the making, something she locked on to the moment she read the article in *Sports Magazine*, the season Noah Riley joined the Tomahawks as a walk-on, having declined to participate in the draft his first year of eligibility. At the time, we were nothing but kids, fresh out of college, and had no clue how to make it happen. Over time, though, she put together a business plan, and it was a solid one.

Still, she needed money to make it happen and had little of it.

She needed connections, and the kind she was after wasn't in our tiny hometown. She needed big city moguls, and I needed to become the person she needed most.

It wasn't easy by any means, but Noel was what

drove me, even if she didn't know it.

Having Noah and Arianna Riley be the ones to invest, and with the *full* amount we needed to keep the integrity of the place we refuse to diminish, isn't Noel reaching for the stars, it's soaring beside them in the sweeping galaxy, where she can touch their tips.

I would bet all I have, Noel slipped away to shed a few tears after our conversation with the happy couple.

Her dream took on an entirely new meaning. This, this is beyond her wildest imagination, to have those most connected, most passionate, share in this journey.

It's like I told her last night, I'm so fucking proud of her.

She's strong and resilient, and mine.

She thinks I came home for a show for business reasons, that when the dust settles and the accounts are full, I'll head back to 'my side' of the country that was never intended to be my home, but she's wrong. She thinks I abandoned her, but she's wrong about that too.

We were never supposed to be apart for so long, and if I have it my way, we never will be again.

CHAPTER 7

N oel

"Miss, you must come inside. There's a blizzard rolling in from the north."

My head snaps over my shoulder, confusion whirling in my mind as I blink back into the now, having zoned out for who knows how long.

The moment I do, my gloveless hands lift to my cheeks, and I realize they burn from the chill.

How long have I been out here?

"Miss..."

"Yeah, shit, sorry." I pull my coat tighter around

me and make my way to the double doors. It had taken a while for the patio to clear out, and the moment I found it free, I eagerly ate up the space. Guess I lost track of time, but the beauty in the quiet a night in the mountains provides will do that to you.

As I step into the building, a group of four men rush out onto the deck, quickly pulling the furniture inside and closing the heavy oak doors behind them.

Peeking at the clock, I find it's almost midnight, and other than a young couple huddled in the corner together, the bar is empty, having likely returned to their rooms to settle before Christmas morning comes.

Thunder jumps outside in that exact moment, matching the echoed pain in my chest as I watch the clock tick another minute closer to December twenty-fifth.

I look to the windows, trying to catch a glimpse of the angry streaks in the skies, but it's too dark to see anything outside my own reflection.

I stare at it a little longer, taking in my pinkened cheeks and the fluff ball my once sleek ponytail has become. My eyes are sloped at the edges, my body and mind weighted. Weary.

Wishing to go back in time...

"I can turn the lights back on," one of the gentlemen offers.

I give as much of a smile as I'm capable of and shake my head. "No, that's okay. I think I'll float around in the lounge outside a while."

"Have a good evening, miss, and... Merry Christmas."

My muscles lock, the hint of pity in his gaze unmistakable, and I give a curt nod, unable to force the pleasantry from my lips.

The bartender tops off my glass on my exit, and with slow movement, I make my way around the corner, stopping short at the sight of Roman asleep in the barrel chair.

His arms are crossed over his chest, his chin pressed to it, a small frown marring his brows, even in slumber.

I'm frozen there, staring at the man as my thoughts ping pong, trying to decide whether I want to wake him or tiptoe past, in hopes I don't. It's frustrating how equally weighed both options seem to be. One day ago, I'd have deliberately woken him by clicking my heels as loud as possible and making a shitty comment, ruining his peacefulness simply out of spite.

How did twenty-four hours of no real conversation, fantastic sex, and tender yet fleeting comments change so much?

Because, deep down, nothing ever really changed for you.

I take a silent, slow step, and then my phone rings. Loudly.

I wince, my eyes flying to Roman, who's staring right at me.

When my phone rings again, I realize I froze in my getaway position and drop my floating foot down, swiftly pulling my phone from my purse.

Who would be calling me this late?

My nerves prickle at the sight of Dina's name, the opening having gone off without a hitch.

"Hey," I answer, bracing for the inevitable bad news.

"I knew you were still up. Meet me at the front desk?"

Roman frowns in question, but I tear my gaze from his and start for the elevator.

"Tell me what happened."

"Nothing happened. All our guests are good, and judging from how deserted it is down here, I'd say tucked in their rooms."

"But?"

"But the sheriff just came in to let us know they closed the roads for the night and won't be reopening them until tomorrow afternoon, *if* they can get them cleared in time."

"Dina," I snap, glaring at Roman when he appears and slides into the small square space, now suffocating me with his divine cologne, mixed with his natural, piney, spicy scent.

I close my eyes, so I don't have to stare at him stare at me.

My cousin laughs lightly. "I'm standing by the elevator, see you in a sec."

Frustrated, I sigh and shove my phone back into my clutch, flinching when warm palms touch my frozen cheeks.

My eyes fly to Roman's.

"You stayed outside too long." Worry settles over his forehead, his fingers spanning wider to offer more warmth.

"How did you know I was outside?"

"Why ask a question you know the answer to?"

Because he was watching me all night but didn't impose.

Because he was worried.

Because he waited…

"Why did you wait?"

He turns our bodies so we're facing each other, and his other hand rises to match his right on my cheek. "You know why, Noel." His tone is too gentle, too broken, like it's spoken from a throat healing from a thousand cuts.

A sob threatens to escape my own, but I'm saved by the ding of the door, and I wrench myself away from him, rushing out and coming to a quick halt at the sight of Dina.

Her eyes widen as she glances from me to the man beside me—he just keeps placing himself *right there*.

"Um—"

"What's going on?" I rush.

Please distract me.

"So, we have a teeny, tiny problem that's not really our problem, but knowing you, you will make it our problem, and really, you should because it's—"

"Dina," Roman calmly interrupts her rambling.

"So, like I told you on the phone, the roads are closed until tomorrow sometime." She looks to me. "And tomorrow, um..." She chews her lip, eyes flashing to Roman briefly.

"The point," I urge her to continue, aware dark

eyes have sliced my way and fully intent on ignoring said eyes.

"Two families were on their way home from a holiday party and got stuck on the road…"

My face falls. "And we're sold out."

Dina nods. "I thought maybe they could just hang out in the lobby or lounge, and they said that was more than enough, but they have kids, and well, tomorrow is… anyway, I haven't said anything to them yet, but I already had Maggie go pack my things. She's taking my bags to her room. Housekeeping is in there getting it ready, so that covers one, but mine's a single bed, so even if they wanted, they can't all squeeze in there."

"Okay." I nod. "Okay, yeah, thank you for that. So, no-brainer. Give the others mine. I can share with you guys."

"Absolutely not."

I ignore the protest of the man at my side and begin backward steps to the elevator. "Send house-keeping, and I'll go pack—"

"They have five kids," Dina rushes.

My feet halt. "Shit."

My room, while a suite, is a single-bed suite, the majority of the space taken up by its theme, drowning you in the memory of choice.

"No problem," Roman quips, and we look at one another. "They can have my suite, and I will share yours."

Panic prickles along my skin, my hackles rising. "Absolutely fucking not!"

His glare is sharp, head yanking back as hurt burns behind his deep, dark eyes.

"What… room do you have, Roman?" Dina cautiously asks.

My head snaps her way. "He is not… no."

I expect him to say he picked Super Bowl or Campus Rush, utterly surprised when he says, "Christmas Day. It will be perfect for the children."

It's as if hands have wrapped tight around my throat, squeezing, harder and harder, until I'm turning blue, seconds from fainting, but I manage to cough through it, swiftly spinning and clamping my eyes closed. The hand still holding my wineglass is numb, but I manage to bring it to my lips, finishing the full glass in a single swallow.

"No." My voice is thick with a rasp, so I clear my throat and try again, facing the pair. "No. Give them your room. You can store your things in bag check and lock up the library as your space for the evening. I doubt anyone will make their way over before you're up tomorrow as it is. The couches in there are cozy and large, or we can bring a roll-away in." I give a curt nod, settling the issue.

"Forget it then."

I look to Roman. "What?"

"I'm with you, or I'm in my room."

"Don't be ridiculous."

His stance widens, and he lifts his chin, speaking to Dina. "The library will be plenty of space for the family. I'm sure they will be more than happy with a large area to themselves."

Dina nods, creases forming along her forehead.

"The library is warm and cozy, sure, has an espresso machine and large windows to look out at the snow, yes. A wood-burning fireplace, duh, but it's the one space free of holiday décor outside of the pine cones and ribbon-bound mistletoe. Your room is the ideal space for a family, considering what day it is."

"I am aware of the *Beauty and the Beast*-inspired sanctuary you created, Noel. Don't forget, I had a hand in this place as much as you did," he bites out, his face blank for the first time tonight. "Your room, or my own."

"It's okay, the family is very sweet," Dina attempts to settle the issue. "They're honestly happy we said they could wait out the storm inside in our lobby. They will be grateful for any given space regardless."

"There are no decorations in there. No red and white. No tree."

"The entire vibe of this place screams, 'Winter Wonderland,' Noel." Dina smiles assuredly. "It's okay."

But the lights and the music, the nutcrackers and tinsel, and reindeer pajamas—all things encompassing the room Roman can offer them.

My heart begins to beat wildly, a little out of control.

I can't.

He can't...

There's just no way.

I'm prepared to say so, but then my gaze is pulled down the hall where a little girl with blonde hair runs, dragging a stuffed snowman behind her. A second child, this one a few years older on her tail, a Santa hat hanging half off her head, falling to the floor.

She stops then, picking it up and slipping it over her curls, and then she looks up. I expect sadness, disappointment—they're stuck in a hotel, and I imagine her to think *what if Santa can't come...*

But the little girl smiles, her two front teeth missing, and she waves. "Merry Christmas!"

Tears prick my eyes, my chin wobbling, and I look to Dina.

She wears a sympathetic smile and nods.

"Be sure to get their sizes and bring some of the PJs down for them."

"Of course," she whispers softly.

I can't bring myself to look at Roman, and just barely manage to say, "I'm in room four-twenty-three." And then I walk away while my muscles still work.

But Roman wouldn't be Roman if he didn't stop me with a firm yet soft grip. His heavy knuckles press beneath my chin, lifting my gaze to his, searching for something beyond the surface. His shoulders fall, and he whispers for only me to hear.

"If having me in your room hurts you this badly, I will stay in the library." He shifts closer, his other hand gripping on to my hip as if the need to touch me, to hold me consumes him. "I'll sleep in the fucking snow if it takes this broken look off your face."

My eyes well with tears, my hands flying up to grip his wrists.

I'm not sure what I intended to do, but he releases me before I'm forced to decide whether I needed the contact just as much.

"Room four-twenty-three."

His frown deepens, but he nods, and this time, when I walk away, he lets me.

Thank fuck for that, because I need a damn minute alone.

Of all the possible mishaps I ran through my mind prior to this weekend, this is the last thing I *ever* expected.

It's absolute worst-case scenario.

Why?

Why did there have to be a storm?

Why did we slay opening weekend by filling every single room this place offers?

Because this place was meant to be magic, but you weren't supposed to become a casualty of it...

I scan my phone over the slot and push the door open, glaring at the sight.

Why did you insist on tormenting yourself?

My plan was to stay away until my body demanded I retreat to my room for the night, where I would allow myself my one day a year to remember, to smile and miss and retrace every detail, and then I'd permit myself to break. To get angry.

To scream without screaming.

To cry without someone around to try and soothe me.

That was all everyone did when the literal man of my dreams left.

Only Dina knew the absolute truth of it all, but no one wanted to let me break or wallow, and eventually, sooner than I was ready for, I pretended it didn't matter. That he didn't matter, and my life wasn't over when all I felt was a dark, deafening emptiness.

Thank God there was work to be done, and if it weren't for the job opportunity waiting for me in Los Angeles, there's a good chance I'd still be living in my pity party.

I step inside my memory and prepare to give myself a mental pep talk before the patchy wall job around my heart is punched through by the very man who forced me to build it.

CHAPTER 8

❄

R oman

THE DOOR TO NOEL'S ROOM IS OPEN WHEN I REACH it. Not fully, and you can't see an inch inside, but open nonetheless, a small bath towel preventing the latch from clicking.

"I would have preferred to wait outside while..." My words fail me as the room reveals itself, my luggage falling to the blush carpet with a soft thud.

I swallow, my eyes bouncing from one tiny detail to the next, the blood in my veins turning to ice as my muscles heat, my brain perplexed, confusing my body with its crossed signals.

I hadn't thought much about her memory of choice until her reaction earlier, having assumed I knew exactly what she'd choose.

Glitz and glam or summer lake house—both incredibly different yet uniquely, perfectly her.

Never once did I expect to walk into the scent of cinnamon and sugar, of pine needles and firewood. Of roasted marshmallows and warm hearth.

Of us.

The Christmas tree sits in the corner, a glittery green box perched on a stool beside it, overflowing with ornaments, waiting to be hung on the softly lit, yet bare tree. The small table for two in the opposite corner has two neatly folded aprons hanging over each chair, a small basket full of sprinkles and icing packets, a fresh batch of Christmas cut cookies sitting in the center with a folded card settled on top reading *Cookies for Santa*.

My throat threatens to close as my eyes blur, and I don't remember moving to the open door of the suite's bedroom, yet there I stand, staring at the bed, the comforter a silky, shiny silver, deep emerald green and red pillows aligned along the headboard, a small stuffed snowman sitting in the center, a tiny present woven tightly in its palms.

My body slumps, falling against the frame as my head meets the wall.

I close my eyes, wetness coating my lashes as I take a deep breath and fall headfirst into that night five years ago.

My pulse pumps wildly as I stare at the woman across the room, dancing softly to the music as she gingerly slides a tray of sugar cookies into the oven, determined not to allow this batch to burn like the last two.

Sneaking my phone from my pocket, I hold it up, snapping a picture the moment she slides the pad of her thumb along her lips, licking the bit of icing stuck to her satiny skin, frowning when I stare back at it, the gleam of a princess cut diamond glittering across my screen, taunting me.

Tainting us.

She glances my way, a teasing scowl pulling at her features. "We said no work tonight. Purely Christmas Eve fun and festivities."

"I don't know, you're working pretty hard on those cookies," I tease, setting my phone on the counter, I make my way to her.

"Working hard not to char them, yes. I doubt Santa likes burned snacks."

Chuckling, I bend, swiftly sweeping her feet out from under her, and cradle her in my arms.

She squeals, arms looping around my neck. "Put me down. I'm way too heavy for this!" she protests, yet snuggles in more.

My grip on her tightens in response, my body humming in pleasure of having her this close. "Hush. You fit perfectly in my palms."

A little glare takes over her face, but it's more playful than anything, and I want to nip at her jaw in punishment.

Lowering her onto the couch cushion, she purposefully falls back into the velvety green blanket she bought for me, reindeer and little bells all over it. She sighs, pretending to make a snow angel out of the oversized couch throw, before hopping up with a clap.

"Okay, let's—" She gasps, dashing toward the wall we taped a picture of a fireplace to, all so she could tack some stockings up beside it, hers already sitting full.

I smirk, and she laughs.

"You little sneak, and here I was waiting for you to stop paying attention to me, so I could slip away to be the first one done, and you already had me beat."

"Get over here. Let's get this tree decorated."

Beaming, she hurries over, digging through the random things we got at the local drugstore—the only place we could find open by the time we tracked down a tree.

We take turns putting ornaments on the tree and tear open a box of Oreo-flavored candy canes, Noel thrusting one toward my mouth when it breaks as she pulls it out.

I take a small bite, my face scrunching at the oddly grainy taste.

"Nasty, right?" She giggles, tossing it back into the now empty box while I lean over the couch to plug in the lights we strung around the tree before dinner.

Together, we step back, laughing at our mismatched Christmas tree.

"My mom would have taken all these down and redid the tree if she saw this."

"My dad wouldn't even look at it, so you win."

Grinning, Noel leans her head on my shoulder and it takes all I have not to wrap my arms around her. After a moment, she sighs, looking up at me through thick, dark lashes. "Thank you for tonight, Roman. I needed this."

My heartbeat thumbs harder as I stare down at her. "Don't thank me for doing something I wanted to do."

"You wanted me to call you crying, then drag you all

around town to find a last-minute tree and decorations, making quick work of destroying your freakishly clean kitchen on Christmas Eve?"

"I wanted to be with you."

Noel's chest inflates, her gaze flicking to my lips for a split second, and then the timer on the stove goes off. Noel clears her throat and turns away. "Let's get the cookies out before they're toast."

My body heats as I stare at her, tracking her every step to the stove and back. Watching as she sets the potholders beside her, smiling down at the candy cane-shaped cookies we finally got right. She places her hands on her wide hips, hips I want to grab hold of and pull into my own, and smiles.

"Holy shit, they're perfect."

"You're perfect."

Her head snaps my way, the smile on her lips slowly falling as she takes me in.

My fucking chest heaves, my skin burning, fingers twitching at my sides as I push off the counter. Every step I take is slower than the last, and her palms flatten on her thighs, chin lowering, but her eyes... those eyes never leave mine.

"And smart." Another step. "Thoughtful and kind."

Creases form along her brow, her head tipping back

a bit as I pause right in front of her, my thumb lifting to wipe them away.

Her eyes close, and she leans into my touch, her mouth ghosting along my wrist, making my voice grow gruff. "Brave and beautiful."

I shift into her, her body made to mold flawlessly into mine, to melt against me. For me.

My thumb grazes along her jaw, slowly sliding along her lower lip.

"So fucking soft..." I murmur, my forehead falling to hers, her mouth so goddamn close.

"Roman, wha..." She swallows, her hands coming up to fist in my shirt.

My hips press to hers, and she gasps at the feel of me, hard against her soft stomach, morality long-fucking-gone, the woman of my dreams right fucking here.

To test her reaction, I drag her lower lip down, my lips twitching when she seeks out the contact. I lean in more, our mouths grazing one another's, and she sucks in a quick breath.

"I'm going to kiss you now, Kitten," I breathe, my mouth instantly falling on hers, my lungs filling with air I didn't know I had deprived them of, senses flooding with cinnamon and spice.

A heavy groan whooshes past me, and I deepen the kiss, my hand tethering in her hair and tipping her head back, tongue sinking into the softest fucking mouth known to man.

She whimpers, tugging on my tee, and every inch of her liquefies for me. Into me.

Because... *of* me.

My free hand comes up to join the other, and I suck her tongue into my mouth, nipping at her with a heady groan. "You're mine. You were always meant to be mine."

Noel turns to stone, and I yank back, looking down at her.

Her brown eyes are wide, horror struck across her features, but those eyes... they're not pointed at me.

They're focused over my shoulder.

Frowning, I glance back.

That's when his fist connects with my jaw.

My head whips from the impact, my lip splitting instantly, small speckles of blood spraying across Noel's face.

She jolts, shouting, and I gently shove her aside as I spin, taking a second hit, before grabbing the asshole by the throat and hauling him backward, slamming him into the counter, trays of cookies crashing to the floor around us.

"You guys, stop!" Noel screams, sobs thickening her voice. "Stop it!"

I release him instantly, swiftly turning to her, my heart breaking as tears spill down her cheeks, her gaze on the mess around us slowly rising to mine.

"Kitten—" I jerk toward her.

"Are you fucking kidding me?!" I'm torn back, and this time, I don't play nice.

I've waited for this for too long. I swing with my elbow, colliding with his jaw and shoving him backward.

He hops up, swiping at the split on his lip, flicking his gaze to the woman behind me, anger and disgust written across his.

Her sobs stab at my gut, and I lurch to the left, blocking her from his view, but his foul chuckle is as damaging as the disdain in his eyes. He walks backward toward the open door I didn't hear him enter through.

"You know what, fuck both of you. I'm out of here."

And then he's gone.

Rigid yet trembling with rage, I whip around to Noel, darting for her, needing to hold her, to check on her, but she throws her hands up and runs away.

She flies into my room, locking herself in, leaving me to pound on the other side.

Minutes turn into an hour, and I droop against the floor, pleading with her to open it and let me in, knowing she's tearing herself apart right now.

I imagine her lying in the center of my bed crying, curled on top of the soft gray comforter, burying herself between the green and red Christmas pillows she insisted I needed when she came over and saw no sign of the holidays in my house. They're extremely feminine for my specific taste, but she smiles every time she comes over and sees them, so they're worth the outrageous twenty bucks a pop.

I'm not sure how much time passes before the door opens, and I fall backward, staring up at a red-eyed, red-cheeked Noel.

But it's not sadness I find. It's anger.

And then my eyes fall to her fingers, to the folded piece of paper hanging from between them.

My face pinches and I jump to my feet, moving toward her, but she only backs up.

"Noel, where did you—" I cut off, my gaze picking up on the small wooden box beside my bed, the lid open, the only item from inside now in her grasp.

"What is this?" she whispers at first, and then she screams it, jerking toward me. "What is this, Roman?!"

"It's a letter."

"Obviously. Tell me it was meant for someone else." She slams it into my chest, hurriedly moving away from me.

I let it fall to the floor, my eyes searching hers. "Do you want me to lie to you?"

"When did you write this?" she demands.

"Tenth grade."

A blubbering cry puffs past her lips, her gaze zeroing in on the tattered, folded and frayed paper on the floor between us, but I keep my eyes locked on her as I recite the words from the page off memory alone.

"I've loved you since ninth grade when you told me to go fuck myself after a football game." My palms sweat as her attention lifts from the old love note crashing into mine.

"Don't," she whispers.

I continue, "I've loved you a long time now. Longer than you'd believe if I told you, 'cause what's a fifteen-year-old kid like me know about love anyway, right?"

Her hand slaps over her mouth, attempting to muffle her cries, but the tears are there, vast and flowing.

"All I know is when I go to bed, I think of you. When I wake up, I think of you, and when I'm not with you, I want to be. This is going to sound crazy, but I'm pretty damn sure you're the girl I'm supposed to marry, so I'm going to do whatever it takes to make you happy. To make all your dreams come true, no matter what that means,

because you deserve that. You deserve it all, so from today until you force me to stop—maybe not even then—I'm going to do whatever I have to do to make sure I'm the guy you want by your side, and when I'm worthy of standing beside you, I'm going to ask you to be mine forever. And you know what, Kitten? You're going to say yes." My eyes move to hers, her lips trembling as I speak the last line. *"But I guess I have to find the courage to ask you out first for any of that to happen, don't I? Love, Roman."*

The air in the room is thick, suffocating. The silence deafening.

My heart fucking shredding as she trembles before me, anger and sadness bleeding from every inch of her.

"You should have told me."

"You were happy with him, Kitten. I couldn't— wouldn't dare—ruin that for you."

Her lower lip trembles, tears staining her cheeks.

"But then this summer, when he asked you to marry him, you looked up at me over his shoulder, and you didn't say yes until I forced a smile. And I knew. I knew for sure you loved me, too. More than you did him. Different from him, but it didn't matter because you were still going to marry him," I whisper, shuffling forward the slightest bit, and that tremble makes its way through her entire body. "But you're not his anymore."

"Roman..."

"You never were, not truly, you—"

"I have to go," she breathes, cheeks streaked with hot tears.

My brows snap together, and I dart toward her, hope and confusion whirling within me, making me nauseous.

"Kitten."

Her eyes fall to the floor, arms hugging herself. "He's already calling..."

I swallow, dread wrapping around my limbs, weighing me down.

She shuffles away, putting as much space between her and me as the room will allow, and slips into the living room.

"Noel, don't go to him." I follow her backward steps with forward ones of my own. "Please. He doesn't deserve your time. Stay with me. It's Christmas Eve."

Her features crumble, lips trembling as she unsteadily opens the door, her gaze flicking to the clock on the wall, the time ticking just behind the twelve. Tears spill down her already stained cheeks as her eyes meet mine. Her jaw sets, and when the words leave her, they're strong. Final.

"Move out of the way."

They're a goodbye.

"If you leave, don't bother coming back."

I don't know why I say it. The moment I do, I want to take it back, but my tongue won't seem to work.

Noel's face falls, pales, and she shrinks into herself.

"Merry Christmas, Roman."

Then she's gone, and I fall to my knees right where she left me.

I blink, and then blink again, the haze before my eyes clearing as the room I painted a soft gray morphs into a stark white one, every element nearly identical to my old bedroom, yet different.

This is our moment, our night. That is what she chose to immerse herself in this weekend, to relive.

A raw memory of what could have been and wasn't.

"Erie, isn't it?"

My head whips toward her rasp, frowning at her bloodshot eyes, clean of the dark makeup she wore tonight.

She sets her towel on the counter as she steps from the bathroom, hair wet and sticking to her back. Noel slowly looks around the space. "Stepping back in time as if nothing has changed, when really, nothing is the same."

She hasn't faced my way, but I track her every step across the room. Her eyes flicking to the little wooden box on the bedside table, not identical to the one I used to own, but that's what it's meant to represent, then quickly fall to the floor as she walks out into the small living space.

My body turns on its own accord, still half slumped on the wall but compelled by a desperate need to keep her in sight.

"This room." She glances around. "It's what dreams are made of. Someone will say I love you for the first time in front of this fire. Someone will have sex for the first time with the man they never want to let go in this bed. And someone will look into the eyes of the person who wants to spend the rest of their life with them and say 'yes.'" Her tone is agonizingly emotionless, creating a sharp sting within me. "It's a strange sentiment, considering the mess we made of the holiday and all it entails."

"Noel—"

"Do you remember what you put in here that night?" she cuts me off, fingers grazing over the hem of the fluffiest point of the stocking hanging on the silver hook above the electric fireplace.

"Kitten—"

"*Do you* remember?" Her hand falls, back straightening as she turns to face me, her expression completely blank. Numb.

My chest cracks a little more. I shake my head.

"Shame." Noel shrugs, walking past me to the mini bar in the corner, where she grabs a half-empty bottle of wine from the fridge. Pouring two glasses, she finally turns, offering one to me. "I wonder about that sometimes."

She takes a sip, holding the other glass out farther, higher, and I force myself to stand, my feet heavy as I make my way to her.

I reach out, and seconds before my fingers meet the glass, she throws the drink in my face, cool, sweet liquid stinging my eyes and dripping down my chin. I blink through it, catching the tremble of her lower lip before she can force it still.

Noel darts away, but I quickly block her escape, capturing her around the middle, swiftly stealing and setting her glass down so I can lock my arms around her tighter.

She fights me, banging her fists into my chest, yanking against my shirt, but it doesn't take long for her forehead to fall forward, her arms to tuck themselves in, subconsciously cradling herself into my protective hold. Soft sobs shake her shoulders, her fists clenching and unclenching my button-up.

Several minutes go by, my shirt soaked and sticking to me from both the merlot and her tears when she finally looks up, brown eyes beaten and begging for something, though I would bet she has no idea what exactly it is she wants.

So I give her a little of what I want her to know. "I thought of you all the time. Wrote letters to you I never sent," I admit. "Bought at least a dozen one-way tickets home, made it all the way to the boarding gate a few of those times, too, but could never bring myself to walk through it. I know you were hurt by what happened, but I think deep down, you know I never wanted that."

Warm tears spill from her eyes, and when I reach up to wipe them away, she allows it, her eyes closing, though only for a moment.

"You were my best friend," she whispers.

"I know."

"And you kissed me."

"I did."

"A week before my wedding."

"A wedding you didn't plan to go through with, to a man you didn't love, who didn't love you."

"To your *brother*."

"To an asshole who took his assistant to a hotel and left you alone on Christmas Eve." Anger and betrayal boils in my blood, sending a flash of heat across my skin. "I've hated him since the day he found the same letter you did, and asked you out the next day, but he stopped being my brother the second he hurt you. Hurting me, I could handle. Hurting you was something entirely different."

"But you hurt me, too. You told me not to come back, but I did. I came back not eight hours later, and you were already gone."

A sharp ache drills into my chest at her words, at my very own haunting memory of watching the woman I finally had in my arms, walk out of them to head back to a man who cheated and felt no shame for it. "Like you, Kitten, I broke that night, too. And I've been breaking a little more each day since."

She winces, guilt drawing her features in as her fingers tighten their hold on my shirt. "I... I must have hurt you all the time, being with him."

"That doesn't count. You didn't know."

Her eyes snap toward the empty tree, her nostrils flaring as she speaks, so low I almost miss it. "I think I did," she admits. "I've replayed so many moments in my mind for years, and I... think I knew, because I felt it. I—"

"You loved me, too," I offer softly.

Noel pulls in a shaky breath, her eyes moving

back to mine. "No… not—" She licks her lips. "Not loved."

My stomach drops to my feet, my hands shooting up to grip the sides of her face. "Noel…"

Her lips twitch slightly, and she whispers, "Don't pretend like you didn't know."

A soft, thick chuckle leaves me, and I press closer. "Oh, I knew, but I wasn't sure you realized how long ago you became mine."

She nibbles on her lower lip. "The night I told you to go fuck yourself after your football game. I felt it, but you never made a move."

"I was a fool."

"Yeah."

We share a small smile, our foreheads meeting at the same time.

"We can't go back, Roman."

"I don't want to go back. I want to go forward."

"It won't be so simple."

"It will." I tip her chin up, staring straight into her eyes. "It is, Noel. No one else matters. Not what they think, what they say, or who they are. The minute I learned you didn't leave me on Christmas Eve to go back to him, but to let him go for good, I planned to come to you—another ticket I bought that went unused. But then I found out about the job you accepted, and I knew you were where you were meant to be. I know the networking the new position would give you all you needed to make this resort happen."

"That's why you fought so hard for our partnership," she whispers as it all clicks.

"Yeah, baby." I caress her cheeks. "I had to find a way to stay close, to be a constant in your life you couldn't forget. It was torture, but I waited until I could walk away from my temporary life in Florida with all I needed to start one with you in LA."

"Last summer was what I had decided. I packed, ended my lease on my apartment, and made arrangements in LA, but when the date came, I was fucking terrified. We were deep into getting the resort ready, and I knew you were stressed. I worried it would block how you felt, leaving only room for anger, so I kept delaying. But let me be clear, I came home *for you.* Not for business or this trip. Not to mess with your head, just to go back to Florida when the holidays ended." My gaze moves between hers. "I came home to tell you how sorry I am, how much I love you, and to ask you to give me what I want. Give me what I want, Noel."

Her chest inflates. "And what is it that you want?"

"I want you, only and always, and I don't want to take it slow. I want to move into your home until we can find one together, and I want an office right next to yours. I want to erase all the insecurities my brother put into your head and erase all the hurt I left you with while you do the same for me. I want to marry you as soon as you'll allow, and I want to have those babies you've always wanted." I pull back, staring at her. "Give me what I want, and I'll give you more than you ever imagined having. I'll love you harder than you knew a man could love, and I'll fuck you better than any man could ever dream."

A thick laugh escapes her, and she sniffles. "You were doing so good," she breathes, both of us chuckling slightly.

"Couldn't leave the last bit out, baby."

"Roman?"

"Hm?"

"Fuck me better than any man could ever dream..."

I groan, walking her toward the bedroom once more. "I'm going to do more than that." Swooping down, I kiss her throat before meeting her eyes once more. "I'm going to rewrite Christmas for us, Kitten, one lost moment at a time," I promise, and not only to her but to myself.

Because like her, Christmas is linked to pain for me now. It has been for the last five years, but no more.

Tonight, we take back what used to be our favorite holiday.

Tonight, we rewrite our memory.

Tonight … we take back *us*.

"Merry Christmas, Noel."

"Merry Christmas, Roman."

With that, I lower my lips to hers.

CHAPTER 9

❄

Noel

I WAKE TO THE SMELL OF COFFEE, MY EYES PEELING open to find Roman slipping from the doorway, a steamy hot cappuccino on the bedside table next to me. My lips curve, and I stretch, slowly sitting up. The blanket falls to my lap and I reach for it on reflex, ready to shield myself once more, but my hand flattens on the fluffy comforter instead, and I bite my lip with a grin as I reach for my coffee, leaving my breasts exposed as I lean back onto the headboard.

The first sip warms my throat and chest, and I close my eyes, inhaling it slowly.

And I realize something right then.

The airiness, the light, willowy feeling whirling in my stomach, in my head and mind… it's peace.

For the first time in a very long time, I'm not eager to jump straight onto my laptop or rush to work. I don't need to busy my mind to keep it from roaming into painful territory. The 'what if' territory.

Quite the opposite, in fact.

I don't want to move from this spot. I want to stay in bed all day with hot coffee and room service.

And it seems I'm not the only one, as moments later, Roman steps inside, his sweats hanging low on his hips, chest bare and carved to perfection, with two large trays in his hands.

He smiles, goes to say something, but then his eyes snap to my naked chest. He groans, muscles rippling with the noise.

"Down boy."

"Oh, my boy is on his way up. Look at him." He glances down, and sure enough, his cock is fighting against the thick cotton.

I laugh, taking another sip, and he squeezes his eyes shut, shaking his head.

"Okay, I can't believe I'm about to say this." He sets the trays down at the foot of the bed, quickly pulling a T-shirt from his suitcase and tugging it over my head. "But I need to feed you before I fuck you, so behave and let me."

My skin flushes in need, but also from his reaction to me, his words.

His desire.

I do as he asks, calling on patience I don't feel and wait for the food to arrive before attacking him. And in return, he does as he says, flipping me onto my stomach, his body blanketing mine from behind.

And with a slight nudge of my knee, he slides inside me in one slow, long thrust.

My chin lifts, neck stretching, and he already knows what to do, his hand coming around and latching on with just enough force to create a block in my airway, forcing me to gasp into the air around us.

He fucks me slow, raw, and to utter perfection.

"I was made to fill you up, Kitten. To scrape your walls and coat you in my cum." His hips jerk harder then, my body bounding forward from the impact, but his grip on my neck holds me in place.

I bite my lip, pressing into his, arching my back higher, and he sings his praise into my ear.

"There you go. Just like a sweet little kitty. Tell me how good I stretch your pussy."

"More."

He growls, releasing my throat and pressing against my upper back until my shoulders fall flat to the mattress, ass high in the air.

He's ruthless in his pounding, heady growls ripping through the air, my moans sharp and cut short as each stab of his cock within me slams against my G-spot, drawing out another.

I start to shake, sweat slick across my skin, and he pulls out, flips me on my back, and slides back in, in seconds.

He grips my chin, holding still until my eyes peel open to lock on to his.

And then his rocks slow, a delectable form of suffering.

I'm so wet, the sounds our bodies make is pure smutty, naughty, and addictive, but the dance between is the complete opposite this time.

His next words are proof of such.

"I love you, Noel. Then, now. Always."

"I love you, too."

"Time to come now." His lips capture mine, and when he lifts my hips the slightest bit, we both find our finale.

And then we take our time reaching a second, at some point landing ourselves in under the warm spray of the shower.

By the time we make it out of our long, steamy shower, it's midafternoon.

We move into the small living room area of the suite, where we do exactly what Roman had promised.

We completely rewrite our memory, decorating the tree that was left bare and the cookies we dug into in the middle of the night when we needed to replenish.

We play board games and order hot cocoa from room service, but as dinner grows nearer, I find I don't want to stay inside the room anymore.

I want to be out among our peers and other guests… together.

I want people to look at us and believe his lie.

That we are engaged and to be married, but then I remember what he said in front of the Rileys.

He called me his wife.

As crazy as it makes me sound when I fought the man with all I had up until last night—or maybe the night before—I want to be.

I've wanted to be for years.

Which is exactly why I push all thoughts from my mind and turn to the man beside me and wait for his eyes to meet mine.

"Marry me."

His brows jump, and he smiles.

And then he tackles me to the bed, pinning my arms over my head. "You did not just ask me what I've fantasized asking you for twelve fucking years."

"I did." I grin. "So what do you say, Roman Dominion? Be mine?"

"Been yours. Will stay yours."

"Is that a yes?"

"It's a fuck yes, Kitten. Now bring those claws out and dig them into my shoulders, because I'm about to punish you for stealing my moment, and it's going to be oh so good."

"Moments can't be stolen anymore, remember? Here, in this place, we give them back. We took our not so merry memory and replaced it with a picture-perfect one."

Roman stares at me, his smirk slow. "You're a

fucking genius, baby, but what I said still stands. Shirt off, nails in my back, legs locked around me. Now."

I don't make him wait, we did that long enough, and we won't do it again.

I was meant to be his, and this man?

It's true what he's been saying, he has always been mine.

For the second time, we're casualties of Christmas, and I couldn't be happier.

I knew Blue Mountain Memories was going to be magic, but I had no idea how magical a rewritten memory would be.

They'll be hills to climb from here, but it's nothing we can't handle.

Side by side.

Hand in hand.

So long as Roman is beside me, every memory made will be brighter than its last.

And if, somehow, it isn't, we'll be right back here, ready to relive it.

Together.

THE END

NOTE FROM THE AUTHOR...

(Curious about Ari and Noah Riley?! Guess what?!
They have a full-length novel that is OUT NOW! Read
Say You Swear TODAY here! Find it on Amazon!)

Gah! Thank you so much
for reading my Christmas short story!
I've always wanted to write one and these two
allowed
me the perfect opportunity for a quick, hot little
holiday second chance romance! I think we'll see
Noel and Roman again. The Blue Mountain and
Memories resort is far to magical not to let some
of my other characters visit, don't you think?…or
maybe even new ones!

And to those of you
who have already read Noah and Ari's story,
Say Your Swear, I hope you enjoyed this little
surprise!

Xoxo, Meagan

Join my private readers group! Search "Meagan
Brandy's Readers Group" on Facebook today!

LOOKING FOR A NEW BOOK BOYFRIEND?

Meet my naughtiest book boyfriend today!
Check out the first chapter of The Deal Dilemma,
a brothers ex-best friend, good girl/bad boy
romance!

…

USA TODAY BESTSELLING AUTHOR
MEAGAN BRANDY

Chapter One

- DAVIS -

"I don't have much time, Baby Franco, so let's hear it."

My lips pinch at the nickname, something he's called me since I was

twelve, the blatant reminder that I, above all freaking else, am the baby of my family—his chosen family, that is until he washed his hands of us, unlike the faded nightclub stamp smeared along his knuckles.

It's whatever. He showed, didn't he?

Sure, he threw himself in the chair across from me, without so much as a one-armed hug, and buried his face in his phone before bothering to look at me, but again, he *is* here, which is more than I can say for the last several years.

Who's counting, right?

It went from seeing him every single day—as one does when their bedroom is directly across from your own—to every other, to once a month, then twice a year, and as of yesterday, he broke an entirely new record for us. It's been almost three years to the day since the two of us have been in the same place, at the same time, and even then, it was for no more than a wave through a dusty Mazda window, which, considering his apartment is less than a ten-minute drive from my own, is telling.

And, apparently, it's not long enough for him if the annoyed sigh pushing past his cherry-ChapStick-covered lips clues me into anything. I'll wait him out, though, because I need his undivided attention in order to ask what I brought him here to ask, so I sit back, waiting for the moody man to look up.

Several more moments, a couple seat shifts, and a flash of a frown later, he finally does. Dark, hazel eyes rimmed in gold meet mine and the hint of irritation rising in my throat simmers.

My gaze softens, a small smile pulling at my lips at the direct sight of my brother's best friend.

Best friend turned foster brother turned ex best friend, that is.

As if his thoughts mirror mine, as if I'm nothing but a reminder of the friendship he lost, Crew winces, flicking his attention away.

"When was the last time you woke up this early?" I tease, glancing at his disheveled hair and last night's hoodie.

A ghost of a grin tugs at the corner of his mouth, but he doesn't quite let it loose. "Been a while." A single beat passes, a second sigh leaving him as he leans forward, arms crossed flat on the tabletop.

Crew's eyes skim over my upper half in a long, slow pursuit, and with each passing second, the deeper the creases along his forehead become. "Your hair's different."

"Oh." Subconsciously, I reach up, running my fingers through the soft caramel-colored strands. "Yeah, I thought it would be fun to go a little darker."

"And shorter."

I nod, squashing my hands between my thighs to keep from touching it again. I had forgotten what I'd changed about myself since the last time he saw me. Chopping my long dirty-blonde hair and going brunette had been a random, rash decision, but I love it. It's short, hanging just above my collarbone, sleek and spunky. My hair never held curls anyway, so now it's ten times easier to jump up and head out the door, not like I ever spent too much time trying to do much more than that, but still. My life had become a monotonous merry-go-round—a boring circle I wanted out of—with new hair, I at least saw something new in the mirror each day.

I also stopped wearing—

"And no more contacts?" It's as if he reads my mind.

An anxious laugh escapes, and I uncross one leg, recrossing them the opposite way beneath the café table.

"My dad has to take me off his insurance when he retires this summer, so I finally gave in and had laser eye surgery."

"You're afraid of needles. And doctors."

My mouth opens and closes, his sharp memory a surprise, and I give a small shrug.

"It was... embarrassingly terrifying but needle-free, and I can't really afford to pay out of pocket right now, so it was kind of the only option."

And I was suitably sedated, plus or minus a Xanax or two.

His brows pull in close, and he gives a slow nod.

For a moment, he simply stares, seemingly lost in thought, but his grumpy little glare comes back, and he looks at his phone again.

If there's one thing about Crew Taylor that drives me mad, it's his ability to live in the in-between, where you show no sign of being happy or glad, mad or sad, serious or playful.

You name it, and his signals are crossed. He can go from calm, cool, and collected to ripping a dude out of a chair with no warning and serving up a fresh fistful. You never know how he feels until the moment he's ready for you to.

He and my brother were opposite in that way.

Memphis wore his emotions proudly. If he was upset, he wanted you to know. Happy, he was eager to share why. On more than one occasion, I witnessed him walk up to a total stranger and ask if they were okay, simply offering them someone to talk with. He would say he felt they needed it, and so there he was, an ear for anyone who needed one. Of course, it worked both ways.

The source of Memphis's anger was made unmistakably clear, but it was Crew who would step in when that happened. It was part of the reason he and Crew fit so well as friends: what one lacked, the other made up for in spades.

Not to say they weren't similar; they were. Their likes and dislikes were matched, be it games or food, clothes or hairstyles. Both were silly and shameless, outspoken, and athletic, so much so, they'd bet on who could get a random girl's number at the fairs or school football games.

Baseball was their game of choice, so they ate up all the attention they could snag under the Friday night lights.

There was so much bait tossed their way; it's a shock they didn't puke.

Pretty sure I gagged a time or two.

But there was always a different kind of shadow that hovered over Crew, and sometimes, he couldn't quite step out from under it.

"I don't have a lot of time," Crew complains with a quick flick of his gaze.

"You don't have work until seven."

His head snaps upright as my lips smack closed, my eyes bulging, but only for a second.

I'm about to apologize when his familiar chuckle warms the air, and this time, while it only holds for a split second, his grin slips free, the small scar along his chin becoming more defined, revealing a new one just left of the other.

Yeah, he's textbook "take me to bed," as the headline would read if you opened a book cataloging men and the thoughts they induce on sight.

He'd be the first photo featured.

His skin is forever tan, body trim yet toned, though looking at him in his hoodie, his shoulders seem to span wider than before. His dark-brown hair is still short on the sides, a pile of lazy waves on top.

Just how I like it.

Crew leans back, crossing his arms. "Been checking up on me, huh?"

"I'd say old habits die hard, but I'm not old, and I don't see this one dying."

His eyes hold mine. "Tell me why you asked me to come here, Sweets."

Sweets.

Man, I haven't heard that one in a long time. Little does he know not much has changed. I still have a solid stash of snacks—all of the sugary nature—in my bag as we speak. That's what he called me before, "Baby Franco," and after, on the rarest occasions, of course. Like when he was drunk and goofy.

Like when he—

The lift of his dark brow snaps me out of my thoughts, and I remember why I called him here.

Not that I forgot. I obsessed over it. *Stressed* over it.

Ate three pounds of chocolate and got sick over it...

Each time I tried to talk myself out of calling him, it worked. I mean, it had been a long time since we talked.

So, I texted him instead.

"Right, so…" I sit up in my chair, folding my hands and laying them on the table, holding his eyes with mine. I square my shoulders, give a curt nod, and grin.

"I want you to take my virginity."

—

Read more HERE:

MORE BY MEAGAN...

Series:

Wicked bad boys and the girls who bring them to their knees...

Boys of Brayshaw High
Trouble at Brayshaw High
Reign of Brayshaw
Be My Brayshaw
Break Me

Standalone Books:

- The Deal Dilemma -
Brothers ex-best friend, good girl/bad boy
romance -
- Say You Swear -
Sports Romance, Amnesia, Second Chance
– Dirty Curve –
Hot College jock falls for the shy little tutor.
– Fake It Til You Break It –
Hottest guy on campus becomes your fake
boyfriend
– Fumbled Hearts –

New girl in town catches the eye of the school playboy

– Defenseless Hearts –

Second chance with the one who got away

– Badly Behaved –

Rich girl falls for the poor punk

Find these titles and more here:
www.meaganbrandy.com/books

WAYS TO STAY CONNECTED...

Purchase EXCLUSIVE merchandise here:
https://www.teepublic.com/user/
meaganbrandy
Private Facebook Group: Meagan Brandys
Reader's group
Facebook Page: Meagan Brandy
Instagram: @meaganbrandyauthor
Amazon Meagan Brandy
Goodreads: Meagan Brandy
BookBub: Meagan Brandy
TikTok: @meaganbrandyauthor

ACKNOWLEDGMENTS

Thank you to the man of my house, who pushed me to write this when I was nervous to try! My books tend to be very long, so a short story is a true challenge for me to accomplish successfully.

To my editors for always being available when I randomly pop in with a book without a proper deadline – or any at all, if we're being real! One day I'll have my shit together for you all. I could not do this without you!

To my team members, thank you so much for riding with me from one genre and trope to the next! This one was a surprise to you as much as it was the world, and you still worked your magic!

And to my readers, for loving my characters so hard that it inspires me to bring you more! Thank you so much for allowing me to do what I do!

ABOUT THE AUTHOR

USA Today and Wall Street Journal bestselling author Meagan Brandy writes New Adult romance novels with a twist. She is a candy crazed, jukebox junkie who tends to speak in lyrics. Born and raised in California, she is a married mother of three crazy boys who keep her bouncing from one sports field to another, depending on the season, and she wouldn't have it any other way. Starbucks is her best friend and words are her sanity.

9 781088 078587